"So, you're giving up?" Les asked, as we walked to school. "On Adam De-Long, I mean."

I shook my head. "No way!" I said. "I'm just changing my strategy, that's all."

Les gave me a funny look. "You know, there *are* other boys in the world. There's Sam Tilden, for example. He's really a nice guy . . . and good-looking, too." There was an odd tone in her voice, but I didn't think anything of it. We always sound a little funny first thing in the morning.

"Maybe he is, but he's not *Adam*," I said. Good-looking? Sam? Sam was just Sam, and I'd never thought about whether he was good-looking or not. Anyway, I couldn't be bothered with other boys. I had to keep working on the Adam problem. I'd think of a new way to capture his attention, I was sure of that.

HEAD OVER HEELS

Susan Blake

IVY BOOKS • NEW YORK

Ivy Books
Published by Ballantine Books

Produced by Butterfield Press, Inc.
133 Fifth Avenue
New York, New York 10003

All the characters in this book are fictitious and any resemblance to actual persons living or dead is purely coincidental.

With special thanks to Carbonell.

Library of Congress Catalog Card Number: 87-91044

ISBN 0-8041-0234-1

Manufactured in the United States of America

First Edition: May 1988

Chapter One

"So what do you want to do?" Leslie Langsdorf asked me. It was Friday afternoon, and we were on our way home from Willow Park High School. "Do you want to go to my house and get something to eat?" She looked at her watch. "It's nearly two hours until dinner, so we've got plenty of time." Leslie always plots how much time she has until the next meal, in case she wants to sneak in a snack or something. Leslie is the only person I know who can sneak snacks all day and never gain an ounce.

"No, let's go to my house," I told her. "I want to show Mom my report card."

Leslie frowned. "I thought you said you got mostly B's. So what's to hurry home about?"

"Yeah, but last time it was mostly C's, so things are looking up. And anyway, one of those B's is an A. In advanced math."

We came to the corner and turned down Lincoln Drive toward my house. "I mean, getting an A in advanced math is really remarkable—isn't it?" I asked. It was going to be really neat to show my whole family that I could be remarkable in *something*, even if it was only advanced math. Mrs. Mitchell doesn't believe in giving lots of A's. Last time, Sam Tilden got the only one, and he practically lives in his math book. I felt lucky to be in the same league as Sam, especially since I don't live in my math book. I just visit it every night for an hour or so.

"You know, Mag," Leslie said, popping her bubble gum sort of absently, the way she does when she's got something on her mind. "I really think you're getting hung up about this thing. About being remarkable, I mean. The rest of us are content with being sort of ordinary and average—you know, we win some, we lose some. How come you're not?"

"Because nobody in my family is average," I retorted, "and that makes me feel *below* average. Let's face it, Les, the only remarkable thing I've ever done was to get my Finding Your Way badge in the Girl Scouts in the same month that I got my Ecology badge. And that was so long ago it doesn't count."

"Oh, come on, Mag, it's not *that* bad."

Les always looks on the bright side of things.

We were walking up the steps of my house, which has this neat old-fashioned porch with gingerbread trim and a porch swing. I sighed and opened the door. "It is, too," I told her. "Look at it this way. If you had a beautiful blond cheerleader for a sister, a swimming champion for a brother, a first-chair cellist for a father, and your local TV station's number-one aerobics instructor for a mother, where would that leave *you*?"

"Way behind and fading fast," Les admitted cheerfully. "Yeah, I get your point."

We went down the hall, and I looked at us in the hallway mirror. There was Les, petite and perky, with her red hair and freckles and that terrific way she has of smiling that lets you know that she's really glad you're there to smile at.

And there *I* was, Maggie the Unremarkable, a completely ordinary and average person. Middling tall, middling slender. Hair that's not quite blond, not quite brown. Unremarkable green eyes, commonplace nose, maybe a little on the short side. Smile that might be okay if it weren't a fraction of an inch too wide.

"You know, Les," I said, staring at myself, "you're right about this hang-up. It's getting so bad that lately I've been starting to wonder if I'm actually invisible. Like, maybe I'm made out of glass or something, one of those transparent models in science class, where you can look through and see the heart and veins and all that stuff."

Leslie giggled. "Hey, maybe you ought to sign on with the circus. You know, the Incredible Invisible Woman. If you did that, I'll bet your family would start paying attention to you." She looked around. "Speaking of family, where is everyone?"

"Rats," I said in disgust as we walked into the kitchen. "Wouldn't you know it? Here I am, with an A in advanced math, and nobody's home to hear me brag about it."

After Leslie dumped her books on the counter and headed for the bathroom, I went to the refrigerator door, which is our family bulletin board. In our house, if you want to know where somebody is, you check the refrigerator door first.

"*Double* rats," I muttered as I read all the notes.

"What's the matter?" Les asked, coming out of the bathroom.

"Well, it looks like Frog's sleeping over at

someone's house. Ellyn went to Orlando on a date. Dad's got an early orchestra rehearsal. And Mom had to go back to the TV studio for some kind of meeting." I opened the refrigerator and peered inside. There wasn't much in there, but I stared at it anyway, as if some wonderfully delicious snack was going to magically appear.

Leslie perched on a stool. "Well, then, you want to come home with me?" She thought for a moment and then shook her head emphatically. "No, on second thought, maybe you don't want to come home with me. Aunt Mildred is coming over tonight, and she's on this really strict diet. So Mom makes everything without any sugar or salt or fat." She closed her eyes briefly. "It's usually pretty awful."

I got the last two cans of soda out of the refrigerator, opened them, and handed one to Les. "That's okay," I said, sinking onto the other stool and trying not to feel sorry for myself. "I guess I can microwave a pizza or something."

"Watch out!" Leslie exclaimed.

"Oh, *fudge*," I said resignedly. I had banged my elbow against my can of soda and knocked it over. "Now I don't even have anything to drown my sorrows with."

Leslie was diplomatically silent while I found a towel and mopped up the mess. She's very nice when it comes to not calling attention to my klutziness. Then she held her can out to me so I could have a sip.

"It's more than just having a good report card and nobody being home to show it to, isn't it?" she asked, in a sympathetic voice. "It's sort of like that old song—'You're Nobody 'til Somebody Loves You'?"

I nodded. Sometimes I think Les is clairvoyant. She can read my mind. "Yeah. Except in this case it's more like you're nobody 'til somebody *notices* you."

"It's Adam, huh?"

I nodded again. "Maybe I wouldn't mind being invisible so much if it weren't for him. He just sort of seems to look right through me."

Les looked as if she knew something I didn't. "Sounds like a major-league crush to me."

"How can I help it? I mean, he's so tall and lean, and he's got that gorgeous dark hair that falls across his forehead and such blue eyes with all those dark lashes, and . . ." I paused for breath. It made me breathless just to think about him.

"Look, Mag, you've been saying the

same things about Adam DeLong every week for a whole month. Isn't it time you got busy and did something about it?"

I heaved a long sigh. "But I am doing something. I mean, I pray a lot. And I keep sort of getting in his way after homeroom so that he'll notice me." I shook my head. "I don't know how somebody can sit only two seats away from somebody else for a whole, entire month and never even see her. It's got to be that I'm transparent, or that he needs glasses—no, contact lenses. Glasses would ruin his looks. There's no other explanation."

"Well, praying won't hurt, I guess. But there's got to be something else besides getting in his way and hoping he'll bump into you." She jumped off the stool. "Listen, I have to get going. But I'm baby-sitting Charles tomorrow night at my sister's house," she said. "Want to come over?"

"Ugh." Charles is Les's three-year-old nephew. His mother named him after Prince Charles of England, but Les and I call him "the Royal Pain." "Yeah, I guess so. Want me to bring my Monopoly game?" It didn't sound like the greatest Saturday night in the world, but it was better than staying home alone.

"Sure. I'll see you later."

"Okay, 'bye."

After Leslie left, I went up to my room. Doodle was there, lying on my pink sweatshirt. Doodle is Frog's dachshund. Frog won him in a drawing at the pet store. I scratched Doodle's ears for a while, and then I read another couple of chapters in the romance novel Ellyn keeps under her bed because she thinks it's too old for me. Then I went back downstairs and found a pizza in the freezer. I put it into the microwave and turned it on high. There was some lemonade, so I took it and the pizza, and went into the living room.

I looked at the clock over the fireplace. It was quarter past six. There were fifteen minutes left of *Aerobics Unlimited*, so I turned on the TV and settled down with my pizza to watch my mother, feeling a little sorry for myself that everybody but me was out doing something interesting tonight. I thought that once I got to high school, my Friday nights would be a little more exciting. But here I was, eating pizza with Doodle sitting beside me on the couch. Some weekend.

When my mother first started doing aerobics on Orlando TV, back when I was in fifth grade, I really got a kick out of watching her. I mean, not everyone's mother is on TV five days a week, looking like a blond, beautiful Jane Fonda, wearing a really revealing leotard. But then the kids at school found out that it was *my* mother and began to tell me how neat it was that I had a mother with a figure like Jane Fonda's. After that, I began to feel kind of funny about it. I mean, other mothers don't wear leotards and do aerobics on TV. Other mothers dress up in suits and go to the office every day, like fathers. Or they stay home and bake cookies. But no, *my* mother has to be different.

Actually, it's not so much that I mind the people in my family being different, if only they weren't so good at what they do. I couldn't have a normal, average sister and brother or mother and father. I had to have Ellyn, who's seventeen and absolutely flawless and pretty nice on top of everything else. In addition to being a cheerleader, she's captain on the debate team and has zillions of dates. Then there's my brother, Frog, who's eleven and very bright and has been winning swim meets since he was five. And of course, there's my father, who plays cello in the Willow Park Orchestra when he isn't being a senior partner in his own law firm. I love them all, honestly I do, but do you see what I mean? All of the Masons—all of them, that is, except me—are truly remarkable.

And me? Well, when Les and I practice cheerleading, I get the motions all mixed up and she has to yell at me. I can't swim (actually, I can't even float). Last year my father gave up trying to teach me the cello because Mrs. Seidensticker, our next door neighbor, complained that it was making her baby cry. I can't even make Adam DeLong look at me when I'm standing right in front of him, for heaven's sake.

As I finished my pizza, I felt even sorrier for myself. On the screen, my mother had finished giving the aerobics lesson and was walking toward the camera. She wasn't breathing hard, even after doing all those exercises, and her shiny blond hair was all smooth and tucked perfectly behind her ears. She had this inspiring, caring look on her face that she has whenever she's about to give her pep talk, which is designed to keep all the women faithfully doing their aerobics, even when it hurts or when they don't have time. I got up to turn off the TV. It gives me an incredible feeling of power to cut my mother off in the middle of one of those pep talks. I didn't *feel* like being cheered up or getting in shape. I was thinking about getting the ice cream in the freezer while I was up.

But then I stopped. Mom was looking straight at me, and her voice had dropped into that quiet, thoughtful tone she uses for our private discussions, when we're talking about serious things, like sex or periods. You know, mother-daughter talk.

"I know what you're thinking," she was saying. "You're thinking that you can't do it. You're thinking that you'll never change the way you are, because that's the way you are. You're thinking that you're stuck with yourself. Aren't you?"

I sat down abruptly on the ottoman in front of the television. Yes, that's *exactly* what I was thinking. Was my mother clairvoyant like Les, too?

"But it's not true," my mother was saying passionately. "You can do anything you want to do, be anything you want to be, as long as you think positively and keep trying. Remember that old saying, 'if at first you don't succeed, try, try again'? That's the way you should approach life. If you don't like the way you look, then change it! If you don't like your outlook on life, change that, too! And if you don't like the way people respond to you, think how you can change that response. Because you can! It's entirely up to you. All you have to do is hang in there and think positively."

The camera pulled back. "And that's all for today, folks," the announcer's voice-over said cheerfully. "Join us again tomorrow for—"

I switched off the TV and sat there with my chin in my hands, watching Doodle eat my pizza crusts, a new determination swelling inside me. My mother was right. I *could* do it! It *wasn't* impossible! As long as I thought positively and hung in there, I *could* make Adam DeLong pay attention to me!

All I had to do was figure out how.

Chapter Two

Saturday mornings around our house are usually a zoo. My father practices his cello upstairs in the study. My mother hangs out in the kitchen, cooking food to have ready for the week and inventing new aerobic routines. It's quite a shock to come into the kitchen and see your mother doing a camel stretch with an egg in each hand and one tucked under her chin. And of course Ellyn is in our room, playing her latest tape at full volume while she folds her laundry or cleans her closet. She's the most organized person I know. Frog watches cartoons in the living room or—well, actually it's better not to ask. With Frog, what you don't know won't make you wish you did.

On this particular Saturday, I was busy, too—for once. I had a lot of thinking to do about what my mother had said the night before on her show. Since Ellyn had the tape on, and Frog had the TV on, and Mom had the radio on, and Dad had his cello on, our house was pretty noisy and not exactly the best place to make any major decisions about changing my life.

So I went into the kitchen to make myself a middle-of-the-morning sandwich. I had an idea: maybe my mother, the counselor, would like to give me the second half of her pep talk, and some details like what sort of changes a girl should make in her life if she wanted it to get better, and how long I should plan on hanging in there.

But she was talking to somebody on the phone. So I made a peanut-butter-and-banana sandwich, only I dropped half of the banana. When I went to look for it, I stepped on it, and it sort of squished into a banana pancake. Doodle, who was asleep on my mother's foot, came over and sniffed at the banana for a minute, but when he found out what it was, he took off for the living room. Doodle doesn't like fruit too much, so when you spill it, he won't get rid of the evidence as he does with, say, roast beef sandwiches or Swiss cheese. So I made a couple of quick swipes at it with the dish towel, and then left. My mother was still on the phone and I didn't want to bug her any more than I already had.

I took my sandwich and climbed the catalpa tree at the back of our yard. I wanted to bring some milk up with me, but it's kind of hard to carry a glass when you're climbing a tree. Believe me, I've tried it. The catalpa tree was like my second home. I used to spend a lot of time there when I was a kid, looking over the fence at Mr. Hutchinson's rabbits and getting away from our constantly busy house. Since I started high school I hadn't climbed it very often, but today it was nice to be there, even if Mr. Hutchinson didn't have his rabbits anymore. It was a nice, private place to go and think about things.

What I thought about was my problem, and how I was going to solve it by thinking positively. As I saw it, my problem was that I was absolutely average, and verging on invisible. If things stayed the way they were, Adam was never going to notice me because he would always be too busy noticing Jennifer Blair, or some other girl. Now, I wasn't saying this in a self-pitying way, I was just stating an objective fact—a fact that, as my mother had said the night before, could be changed.

But how could I change it?

It wasn't any good trying to talk to Adam

during homeroom period, because Jennifer was always around. And I couldn't stand next to him in the lunch line because he had lunch at a different period than I did. Maybe I could wait for him after his last class, end up outside his classroom sort of by accident, and casually walk along beside him to where he caught his bus. But I gave up that idea in a hurry. After the last class, it's like the last stampede at our school, and people who don't run out to their bus have a tendency to get run *over*. I'd be strolling along, Adam would jog past me, and then I'd get hit from behind by the entire sophomore class.

I sighed and munched the last of my sandwich. Maybe I could. . . .

"Hey, Mag, what're doing up in that tree?"

I leaned over. Frog was standing beside the large trunk, looking up at me. His hair was as blond as Ellyn's and curly, and he still had a tan from summer. Life was so unfair, sometimes.

"Would you be a good little brother, Frog, and get me a glass of milk?" I asked.

Frog stuck his hands in his pockets. "What'll you give me?"

"I'll loan you my Monopoly game for an

evening," I said. "Only not tonight." Tonight I was taking it to Les's sister's house to baby-sit.

Frog shook his head. "I don't want it. How 'bout giving me a quarter," he said firmly. Frog is always looking for ways to earn money. He's the wealthiest eleven-year-old I know.

I frowned. "How about if I give you a dime?"

"Twenty cents."

"Frog, it's only a glass of milk. It's not like I'm asking you to risk your life for me, ya know. And—"

"Margaret!" Ellyn was calling me. She's the only one in our family who calls me Margaret.

"What?" I yelled back.

"Where are you?" She came out onto the back porch.

"Why?"

"Where *are* you?"

"I'm up in the tree," I said, "trying to get a little privacy."

"Okay, then I'll do it for fifteen cents," Frog said. "That's my last offer."

"Mom says to come mop the kitchen," Ellyn called.

"But it's not my turn!" I yelled. "I did it last Saturday. It's your turn."

"But I can't do it today," Ellyn said. "I've got to go to cheerleading practice." The screen door banged behind her. There was silence for a while from the back porch, and I began to think that maybe if I just stayed up in the tree long enough, everybody might forget about me and the kitchen floor and let me get back to developing my new positive attitude. But I wasn't that lucky.

"Maggie?" It was my mother, speaking in her reasonable tone. "Maggie, I'd really appreciate it if you'd get in here and mop this floor. Weren't you the one who smashed the banana?"

"Fifteen cents?" Frog asked hopefully.

"Go jump in a lake," I snapped, climbing down.

Mopping and waxing the kitchen floor isn't my idea of a fun way to spend Saturday morning, but I will say this for it, people do stay out of your way. Nobody wants to bother you for fear of being asked to help.

So I tried to think of some new ways to get Adam's attention. I'd already gone through a long list of things—such as bribing the kid who had the locker next to his to trade with me, and riding my bike past his house three times a day—when the phone rang. I couldn't reach it because I was waxing, so I just let it ring. It was never for me, anyway. It was always for Ellyn or someone else. The only person who ever called me was Les, and she was probably out clothes-shopping or something, not stranded in the kitchen with a mop and a bottle of floor cleaner.

"Will somebody please answer that telephone?" my father yelled.

"I can't get it, the floor's wet!" I yelled back. "Frog, answer the phone." Frog didn't say anything. The phone kept ringing.

There was some muttering from upstairs, and then the phone stopped ringing. After a minute, the hall door opened and my father stuck his head in. Half of his face was covered with shaving cream, and he had a razor in one hand. In the other was the phone.

"It's for you, Mag," he said.

"Can you hand it to me?" I asked meekly. "The floor's wet."

He stretched across the waxed part of the floor, gave me the phone and left, shutting the door loudly after him.

"Hello," I said.

"Hi, Maggie. It's Sam Tilden." Sam is the

genius in my advanced math class. He's also in my homeroom. "What are you up to?"

"I'm writing a letter to the president to complain about having to mop the kitchen two Saturdays in a row," I said bitterly. "I'm asking for a hearing before the National Labor Relations Board."

"That's good. Tell the president you know me—it might help." There was a pause, and Sam cleared his throat. "Uh, listen, Maggie. I, uh . . . somehow I missed the assignment in math yesterday. Did you get it?"

I was surprised. Sam Tilden missed the assignment? Mr. Wizard of advanced math 207? "Well, yeah, I did, as a matter of fact," I said. "We're supposed to read the rest of Chapter Six, and do all the study problems that have to do with the compass—you know, all those weird angle and degree problems." Then I thought of something. "Say, listen, Sam, can I ask you what grade you got in math this half-term?"

"I got an A. Why?"

I cleared my throat. "Oh. Well, I sort of got one, too," I said modestly.

"Oh, yeah? Hey, that's great, Maggie! Mitchell's pretty stingy with her A's, sort of like the gold stars old Prunepits used to dole out in third grade. Remember?"

I grinned reminiscently. I once had to do a week's worth of detention for forgetting that Prunepits's real name was Mrs. Prunetz. After that, I didn't get any more gold stars. "Yeah," I said. "I remember."

There was another pause. Finally, Sam said, "Well, thanks for the info. Good luck with your mopping," and hung up.

"Now, that was nice, I thought, as I squeezed the suds out of my sponge mop. It felt good to have *somebody* congratulate me on my A. And I hadn't thought of old Prunepits for years.

The rest of the floor seemed to go a lot faster.

I don't know who Les's sister is going to get as a baby-sitter for Charles when Les starts going out on dates every Saturday night. She probably wouldn't have trouble getting a sitter, *once*. But she'd never get anyone to come back, that's for sure. Les says that her mother makes her father go square dancing every Saturday night just so they won't be available to sit with him.

"Where is he?" I asked, looking around cautiously when Les let me in. The Royal Pain has a trick of hiding behind the door and jumping out at you when you're not expecting it.

Les beamed. "He's in bed already."

"Already?" I asked in disbelief. "It's only seven. That kid doesn't go to bed until midnight."

"Yeah, but tonight's different. Tonight I bribed him."

"What with? He finally gave up his bottle six weeks ago, didn't he?" Everybody had been convinced that Charles was going to graduate from high school with his diploma under one arm and his baby bottle under the other.

"Tapioca pudding," Les said. "He *loved* it. He ate two bowls of it, and then he went straight to bed."

"Tapioca pudding?" I looked interested. "Is there any left?"

"A lot. We can have some later, if you want. Did you bring your Monopoly?"

We settled down in the living room with the TV on and began to play Monopoly. By ten o'clock I had added Reading Railroad to my other three railroads and was feeling pretty rich, but Les was almost broke.

"So, how about a pizza?" she asked, when she landed on Pennsylvania Railroad. "There's one in the fridge. Or we could have some pudding, if you want."

"Sounds great," I said. There was a thump from the direction of the kitchen, and Les looked up.

"What's that?" I asked, counting my money and wondering if I ought to buy another house for Marvin Gardens.

"I guess I'd better go see," Les said worriedly. She put her two fifty-dollar bills down on top of her cards, and then looked at me. "Could you come with me?" Really, Les is *such* a chicken. Not about the stuff I worry about, like school and makeup, but about the things that go bump in the night. She absolutely hates scary movies.

We went down the hall toward the kitchen. There was another thump. We opened the door and poked our heads in. There, squatting in front of the open refrigerator, was Charles. He was wearing his yellow pajamas, and there was a big bowl of tapioca pudding in front of him. Correction—an empty bowl. Most of the pudding was in his hair and on the front of his yellow pajamas, although there were a few cups' worth of it smeared all over the floor. It looked as though he had been skating in it.

"Pudding!" he chortled delightedly, holding up his spoon.

"Give me that!" Les ran to him and grabbed the bowl.

"He's finished it off," I observed. "Looks like we'll be having pizza, after all. Good thing he can't reach the freezer."

"Oh, my gosh," Les said, horror-struck. "Do you suppose all that pudding is going to make him sick?"

"Pudding," Charles said again happily, and burped. "Yummy, yummy."

"Well, it's your fault," I told Les. "You're the one who turned him on to tapioca pudding." I walked across the room to the counter and sat down on a stool. The floor was sticky. Spilled tapioca was even worse than squashed banana.

"More pudding," Charles demanded crossly, looking at the empty bowl.

"There's no more pudding," Les told him. "You ate it all."

"Gone?" Charles asked, with a woeful look.

"All gone," I assured him. "It's time to go to bed."

That did it. The Royal Pain threw one of his famous tantrums, and it took us nearly an hour to wash the pudding out of his hair, button him into clean pajamas, and convince him to go to bed. After we read two stories to him from his favorite Peter Rabbit book, he finally fell asleep, looking cute and completely innocent in his fire-engine pajamas.

"I guess," Les said wearily, when we went back to the kitchen, "that we have to mop the floor now. We can't leave a mess like this for my sister to find."

"Well, don't look at me," I said, backing away. "I've already mopped *one* kitchen today."

Twenty minutes later, Les had finished the floor and I had made salad to go with our pizza. We went back into the living room and sat in front of the television. There wasn't anything all that great on, so we decided to watch a rerun of *Star Trek*. I was pretty sure I'd already seen the episode before, which was pretty amazing considering I've only seen the show four times in my life. It just figured that it had to be the same one. I was sort of wishing that I'd stayed at home by myself after all.

"You know, I don't think that I'll ever have children," I said, around a mouthful of pepperoni. "Baby-sitting the Royal Pain has sort of taken away my interest in motherhood."

"I know what you mean," Les said absently. She was staring at the TV, watching Scotty beam Captain Kirk out of the scaly clutches of the forces of evil.

After I finished eating, I wiped the grease from my hands and picked up a book from the coffee table. It was on square dancing, and I put it back down again about a minute later. I've never been a fan of square dancing. It's a little too cutesy for me. I just can't see myself doing jigs and do-se-dos in public. I picked up a fashion magazine and began to leaf through it, looking at the advertisements and wondering if I would ever be tall enough, thin enough, and *brave* enough to wear any of those clothes.

But as I looked at one picture, an idea burst on me, like a revelation or an inspiration or one of the words that ends in *tion*.

I knew how I was going to get Adam DeLong to notice me.

Chapter Three

When I showed Les the picture and told her my plan, she seemed a little doubtful.

"It's not exactly your style, is it?" she asked, staring at the photo with a perplexed look on her face. "Have you ever owned a pair of hot pink boots? And that long, tight skirt, won't it be hard to walk in? Florida isn't exactly the place for turtlenecks, you know. You're going to roast in it. And what about the hair? I mean, it's so spiky. Your mom will have a fit if you mess up your hair like that. And you'll never get away with that makeup—not here in Willow Park."

"Yes, but look at the caption," I said, pointing it out to her. "It says that this is what everybody's wearing in Los Angeles. And that's where Adam comes from, isn't it? So maybe it does look a little unusual, to our eyes. I mean, Willow Park isn't exactly the fashion capital of the world."

"Yeah," Les said. "That's my point. In fact, I'd say that we're pretty conservative around here. Preppy, almost." She turned the magazine over and looked at the front cover. "Furthermore, this magazine's almost two years old," she pointed out. "Styles change pretty fast. What if this sort of thing is out-of-date in L.A. already?"

"I don't care," I said. The more objections Les had to my idea, the more convinced I was that it would work. "I've got to do *something*. And so what if it isn't my style? So what if Willow Park is conservative? Adam won't notice me unless I stand out from the crowd and look different, and this is as good as anything else." I looked at her. "So how about going shopping with me? I need to look for a pair of pink boots."

Les stared at me. "You're really serious, aren't you."

"I've never been *more* serious," I said. I looked at the magazine. "You don't think your sister would mind if I tore out this page, would she? I need it for reference."

Monday morning was the same as any other morning in homeroom. I was already in my seat when Adam came in and sat down, but I got up casually and sauntered over to the window right in front of his desk pretending I wanted to check on the weather or something. As I went by, I looked down at him and said, "Hello, Adam," in the sexiest voice I could manage.

"G'morning," he mumbled, working furiously at his algebra homework. He didn't even look up.

I paused for a moment, while my fingers considered reaching out to touch the dark hair that curled on the back of his neck, just above his blue shirt—tenderly, of course just one tiny, but ever so meaningful touch. I noticed that I was breathing harder. Should I say something else? Something simple and to the point, like, "Excuse me, I love you"? But no, it wasn't right to distract him from his homework.

Just then, Jennifer walked in and sat down, and Adam looked up and flashed a smile at her, and there was that dimple, that wonderful dimple, and my heart beat harder.

"Hi, Jennifer," he said, and closed his algebra book.

I curled my fingers into a fist and went back to my desk. Whatever it took to get Adam's attention, I was ready to pay the price.

* * *

Les and I really enjoy going shopping, even if we don't have a lot of money. Actually, Les has more money than I do, because her sister has to pay her a special fee to baby-sit the Royal Pain. But I only get five dollars a week allowance, if you don't count lunch money. Still, I'd been saving, and if I threw in my birthday money and got an advance on the next two weeks' allowance, I figured I had enough to buy my new outfit.

We must have gone into a dozen stores in the mall before we found the pink boots. Oh, there were plenty of boots—blue ones, black ones, purple ones—but no pink ones. When we finally found them, they cost a whole lot more than I thought—thirty-two dollars—and the heels were a little too high, compared to the Topsiders I usually wore.

"You're going to wear these to school?" Les asked dubiously. "What about after phys ed class? It'll take you another hour to lace them up."

"Les, you're too practical," I said, which is so true. She likes to try different clothes on, but she always buys the same thing—blue jeans and big shirts.

"I know." Les sighed dramatically. "It's my one failing."

After I paid for the boots, we went to Burgers Bizarre and bought two avocado-and-onion burgers and counted what was left of my money. I only had fifteen dollars.

"Are you really sure you want to go through with this?" Les asked, munching on her burger.

"I'm sure," I said. I took out the picture and looked at it again. It was beginning to tear along the creases, where I'd folded it and unfolded it.

"Well, my sister's got this black skirt that might work. I don't think she wears it anymore, so you could probably borrow it."

"Terrific!" I said enthusiastically. "I was looking in Ellyn's drawer last night, and she's got some pink jewelry that ought to do. So maybe this isn't going to cost as much as I thought." I finished the last of my avocado-and-onion burger. "So all I need is a black turtleneck. Let's go see if we can find one."

Finding a black turtleneck in Florida, especially one with really skinny sleeves, isn't exactly easy. I don't think people *wear* turtlenecks down here, since it's pretty warm and humid. But we finally found one, in the leotard shop. There was only one problem, though. It was pretty revealing. I mean, it sort of stuck to my skin in a very clingy, show-off-your-shape kind of way.

"This is all right," I told Les, turning in front of the mirror and hunching my shoulders forward. "When I get the vest, it'll cover me up. What do you think?"

"I think if you wear that leotard top to school," Les said grimly, "the school board will vote 'yes' on the dress code. Right after they have you arrested for indecent exposure."

"Les! It's not *that* bad," I protested. "You're just chicken."

"Cock-a-doodle-doo," Les said.

After I'd paid for the leotard top and counted the four dollars and thirty cents I had left, I could see that I was going to have to change my strategy. Anyway, it was nearly five o'clock, so we went outside to meet Les's mom, who'd agreed to pick us up—only if we were on time. If we were late, she was going to make us take the bus home. I hate not being able to drive.

The next day after school, Les and I took the bus to the Salvation Army store. It's this really neat secondhand store, where you can buy old records and dishes and junk. They also have clothes, but everything's just sort of thrown on hangers all over the place. It must have taken nearly an hour before I found a vest that was my size and didn't make me look like my grandfather.

"Here it is," I said triumphantly, holding it up. "And it's only two dollars."

"It looks like it's worth two cents," Les said, wrinkling her nose. "What color would you say it is?"

"Purple," I said. "Mostly." I turned around and looked at the belts hanging on the wall. "And here's a wide pink belt that ought to go pretty well with the boots. And over there's a scarf. And they're only fifty cents apiece!"

At the counter, the woman took my three dollars and put my purchases in a bag. "Getting your Halloween costume together?" she asked cheerfully. "My children always go trick-or-treating for UNICEF."

Les snickered.

On the way home, we stopped at a drugstore and I looked at the rest of the things I needed, and figured out how much they cost. Six dollars and eleven cents, including tax. The trouble was, I had less than two dollars left. I thought for a moment of how much all this was costing and whether or not it was worth it. Then I thought of the way Adam's hair flopped across his forehead. It was worth it.

"All I need is five dollars," I told Frog. "I'll pay you back out of my next allowance. Honest." Actually, I wasn't being completely honest, because I'd gotten so many advances that my next allowance wouldn't be next week—it would be next year.

Frog looked at me. "What's it for?"

"You'll see."

"Well, okay, but I'll have to charge you interest. Say, a quarter a week."

"That's robbery!" I squawked.

Frog got up. "Take it or leave it," he said loftily.

"I'll take it," I said with a sigh.

It was Friday night, and I packed all my stuff into my big tote bag—the boots and the top and everything else—and went over to Les's house to spend the night. I couldn't do what I was going to do at my house, because there's just no privacy. Since Les is the only kid at home now, and her parents were going out, we'd have the whole house to ourselves.

"Did you get the skirt?" I asked as we went up the stairs to Les's room.

Les nodded. "I found it. It looks kind of tight to me, though. And it's got this long slit up one side."

"Perfect." I unloaded all my stuff onto her bed and poked through the bag from the drugstore. "Mind if I use your shower?"

"If you're going to wash something," Les said, giving the vest a troubled look, "why don't you use the washing machine?"

"I want to wash my hair, dummy," I said. I showed her the shampoo-in hair coloring I'd bought with Frog's money. "I'm going to use this. And to make sure that the color doesn't fade, I bought this." I pulled out a spray can of hair coloring. "I'm going to keep it in my locker at school."

"But it's *pink*!" Les exclaimed.

I nodded. "I know the model in the picture didn't have pink hair, but I thought it would look really jazzy, with all that pink jewelry and stuff. Can I borrow your blow dryer?"

Les gave me a very serious look. "Maggie Mason, are you sure you know what you're doing?"

"Well, basically," I said, looking at the

bottle. "All you have to do is follow the instructions and—"

Les threw up her hands. "I give up," she said. "I'm going to watch TV. Call me when it's over."

"But I thought you were going to help," I protested.

"I can't stand to watch," Les said, and went downstairs. "You know how much I hate scary movies."

Chapter Four

Once I got over the shock of actually seeing pink streaks in my hair, I started to enjoy myself. It was cool seeing the way the gel made my hair stiff, and my bangs, all spiky. When I was finished doing my hair and began putting on my new outfit, I could hardly believe the change. Of course, Les's sister's skirt *was* kind of tight; if it wasn't for the slit up the side, I knew I'd never be able to climb the stairs at school. And the vest didn't exactly cover up the leotard top, and I looked a little bit like a singer in a rock-and-roll band.

But the belt did match my new boots, and even if the scarf didn't quite, I figured it would provide an interesting contrast. Ellyn's pink beads and pink earrings really electrified the whole thing. The earrings were big dangles, and in order to keep them on I had to screw them so tight that they sort of hurt my ears. Still, if it would get Adam's attention, who cared about a little pain?

I stuck the picture, which by now was half-torn across the middle, into Les's mirror so I would know how to put my makeup on. I had grabbed some makeup from the drawer in my mother's bathroom. She has to wear studio makeup in front of the TV cameras, and she brings a lot of it home. I had found some glittery pink eyeshadow, and some terrific plum-colored lipstick, and I really had fun playing with the violet mascara.

The effect of the makeup was kind of startling, actually. But it went with the outfit, which I had to admit was also kind of startling, now that I saw the whole thing all put together. But I had accomplished one thing for sure. I was no longer invisible.

I went downstairs and stood between Les and the TV set.

"How do you like it?" I asked, posing. "It's just what I wanted," I added, when all she did was stare.

Les kept on staring for quite a while. "Yes, it certainly is something," she said finally.

"I don't understand," Les said, as she pulled on her jeans and her big shirt, "why you think you have to wear that outfit today. Today's Saturday."

"It's very simple," I told her. "I have to get used to it. I mean, if I'm going to pull this off, I have to be graceful, and it's kind of hard to be graceful in a tight skirt and high-heeled boots. Without practice, that is."

"Oh," Les said. She ran a brush through her hair while I put on Ellyn's earrings. The gel was still doing its job, and my hair was as stiff and spiky as it had been the night before. You couldn't even tell I had slept on it.

"You know," Les said thoughtfully, "there's something you haven't thought about."

"What's that?" I asked, lacing up the boots. Les had been right about one thing. It was going to take *forever* to put on my boots after P.E. Maybe I could get out of class somehow. I could tell the nurse I sprained my ankle in my new boots.

"Well, you spent so much money on those boots and everything, you can't afford to put together another one of these outfits," she replied, a little too cheerfully, I thought. "What are you going to wear on Tuesday?" She pointed at my feet. "You don't have very much that'll go with pink, and you certainly can't wear black every day."

"Oh, I don't know about that," I said, tossing my head confidently. "Maybe it'll get to be my signature. You know, my own personal fashion statement. Maybe I'll even start a whole new trend at school. Black is back."

Much as I hated to admit it, though, Les was right. I didn't have anything else to wear with the pink boots, except the pink sweatshirt that Doodle liked to sleep on. But I'd worry about that when the time came. In the meantime, it was kind of neat to think about my setting a fashion trend at Willow Park High School. Not many freshmen could do that, I told myself. The whole school would notice me!

Les just shook her head, kind of sadly, and we went downstairs and cooked a couple of eggs for breakfast.

I was glad that I just lived around the corner. Let's face it: My new outfit wasn't the kind of thing you'd ordinarily see on the streets in Willow Park.

Of course, Adam, sophisticated guy that he was, would appreciate my outfit immediately, not like the preppies in town, who'd probably think it was *too* fashionable. I could just imagine Adam turning away from Jennifer and his algebra book when he saw me. His eyes would light up with recognition and his dimples would flash. "Maggie," he'd say wonderingly, "that's a *terrific* outfit! I never expected to meet someone so stylish and chic in Willow Park! Say, how about getting together for a soda after school? Just the two of us," he'd say with a pointed look at Jennifer.

I came up the front walk, carrying my tote bag. From the front upstairs window I could hear the sounds of my father's cello. He must have been sitting right in front of the window. Frog was on the front porch in his swimming trunks, adjusting something on the strap of his rubber goggles. He glanced up.

"We don't want any today, lady," he said, and went back to working on his goggles.

"Don't be so darned smart," I said.

"My mother doesn't let me talk to strangers."

"Your mother shouldn't let you talk, period."

I opened the door and went into the hallway. Inside, the cello wasn't quite as loud, but you could still hear it, low and mournful-sounding.

Frog put his goggles on and followed me down the hallway. "Is *that* what you wanted the five dollars for?" He shook his head. "I think I should up the interest rate on our loan. Thirty-five cents a week. After all, I have to look at you."

Ellyn came down the stairs. Her blond hair was rolled up in little colored curlers. She looked like somebody's mother, not a cheerleader.

"Listen, Margaret, I know it's my turn to do the kitchen, but I just got this call from Richard and he wants to—" She broke off and stared at me. "Margaret? Is that you?"

"Her mother doesn't let her talk to strangers, either," Frog told me.

"Margaret?" Ellyn asked again. Her voice rose to a squeak. "Margaret, what have you done to your hair?" she cried.

"It's pink, isn't it," Frog observed cheerfully. "And it stands up real good. Did you use glue or paste on it?" he asked me.

"And that *top*!" Ellyn exclaimed, her eyes moving from my hair to my chest. "And that belt! And—" She put her hands over her eyes when she got down to my boots.

"What in the name of heaven is all this ruckus?" my father demanded from the top of the stairs. "All I ask on Saturday morning is a little peace and quiet so I can practice my cello, and what do I get? I get—"

"Pink hair," Frog told him.

"Pink hair?" My father came halfway down the stairs and stood behind Ellyn. When he saw me, he gulped. He stood there for a minute, staring, as if he weren't quite sure whether to believe what he saw. And then, without saying anything, he turned around and went back upstairs. After a minute, the cello started up again, even more mournful than before.

"Did I hear Maggie come home?" my mother asked, coming out of the kitchen. Doodle was at her heels.

"Will you look at this, Mom?" Ellyn said dramatically.

Mom looked. So did Doodle. He sniffed my new boots once or twice, and then turned around and went into the kitchen, his tail drooping.

"We could always tell people that she's being treated for temporary insanity," Frog suggested. "Nothing serious, and the doctor says it doesn't run in the family."

"Mom," I said plaintively, "will you make them shut up! I mean, what right have they got to tell me how I should look?"

"Come on, Maggie," Mom said, putting

her arm around my shoulders. "I just made some cookies. You can have one and tell me"—she glanced at my boots—"where you got the idea for your outfit."

I felt relieved. My mother may look like Jane Fonda, but in my opinion, her best quality is her ability to understand people. We went into the kitchen.

"Well, to tell you the truth," I said, hitching up my skirt so I could climb up onto the kitchen stool, "I got the idea from *you*." Doodle was under the table, and he barked at my boots. Maybe it was something about the way they smelled, or maybe he just liked pink.

Mom looked somewhat startled. "From me?" she asked. "You got the idea from me?"

"Yes." I reminded her of her pep talk that day and what she'd said about making changes.

She handed me a saucer of cookies and a glass of milk. "I see," she said thoughtfully. She looked very serious, but there was a smile behind her eyes. "Is there any special reason why you felt that you needed such a radical change?"

"Well, yes." I hesitated. "But it's sort of a long story. Are you sure you want to hear it?"

"We've got plenty of cookies," Mom replied encouragingly.

So I told her about the way I'd been feeling, about being utterly unremarkable in a family of people who were always doing remarkable things. And then I told her about Adam and how terrific he was, and about feeling transparent, and about my idea to attract his attention by dressing like the girls he was used to seeing back home in California.

"I see," Mom said. She stood up and put her hands on her hips, surveying me. "Well. You're not invisible anymore. He'll have to notice you now." She cleared her throat. "But would you mind if I made one or two suggestions? About makeup, I mean. And maybe about that vest? I think I have something in my closet that might look a little more—well, it might match the pink in your boots a little better."

I sighed happily and took another cookie. My mother is very understanding.

Chapter Five

Mom and I did a little work on my outfit and makeup, and she did something that toned down the pink in my hair and made it a little less starchy. When she was finished, I was pleased. I didn't look exactly like the model in the photograph, of course, but the overall effect wasn't bad, considering.

On Monday morning, I got up early and got dressed. Les came by and we walked to school together. I noticed that she kept her eyes straight ahead, though, and she talked very fast. I didn't say much. I was too nervous. I kept looking at what people had on. It was very, very preppy. If the magazine was right about what was *in*, Willow Park was really *out*. I'd never realized before exactly how conservative we were.

In fact, by the time we got to school, I was so nervous that I didn't go straight to homeroom. Instead, I went into the girls' bathroom and stayed there in one of the stalls with the door locked, until the last bell. Then I hurried as fast as I could, in my tight skirt—which wasn't very fast—to homeroom, and went to my seat.

Being late hadn't been a very good idea, because everybody was already sitting down, which meant that they could get a good look at me. Sam Tilden glanced up from his book, looked very surprised, and then glanced down again, with a little smile. From somewhere in the back of the room I heard a long, low, wolf-whistle, and I could feel my face getting red.

Mr. Harmon, who was taking roll, glanced up quickly. "Oh, hello," he said absently, and then did a double take. "Maggie?" he asked. "Maggie Mason, is that you?"

"Yes, sir," I said. "It's me." All the people who hadn't stared at me when I came in turned to stare at me now.

"Oh," he said, blinking. "Yes, I see. Yes, indeed." And then he went on taking the roll.

After class, I hung around outside the door until Adam came out. Then I sidled up to him. My heart was pounding, my hands were sweating, but I managed to smile.

"Hi," I said.

"Uh, hi," Adam said. He looked at me. "Sort of, uh, changed your style, huh?"

He'd noticed! My plan had worked!

"It gets boring," I said, tossing my head, although my hair didn't move at all when I did, "for girls to wear the same style of clothes all the time. People should experiment more, be a little more bold and up-to-the-minute. Don't you think?"

"I wouldn't know," Adam said in a brisk tone, "never having been a girl."

He was funny, too! I felt as if I were going to faint. We were having a conversation! But what should I say next? It had to be witty and exciting. I cleared my throat, wishing I'd made a list of interesting things to talk to Adam about.

"Well, it seems to me . . ." I began, figuring that by the time I got to the rest of the sentence, I'd probably have thought of something to say.

But I didn't get to finish my sentence. Jennifer stepped up between us, tucked her hand cozily through Adam's arm, and then turned to me.

"I like your outfit, Maggie," she said sweetly. "It's so *original*. I'll bet nobody else at Willow Park has ever thought of wearing an outfit like that to school."

I just stood there for a second and tried

to think of an answer. The trouble with Jennifer is that in addition to being pretty and popular, she's nice, too. Only sometimes she comes out with things that could be either sweet or sarcastic, depending on which way you take them. By the time I figure out which, it's usually too late for an answer. She and Adam strolled off down the hall together as I tried to keep from teetering on my heels.

By lunchtime, I was sorry I'd ever seen that picture in Les's sister's magazine. True, I had gotten Adam's attention, but only for about thirty seconds. And the price I had to pay for thirty seconds' worth of conversation with Adam was endless hours of curious looks and whispers from everybody else at the school.

In English, one of the girls asked me with a giggle whether I was going to sue the beauty salon that had done my hair. In the hall, between English and math, a boy came up to me and asked me for directions to the costume party. And in math, a kid wearing some of those idiotic plastic vampire teeth came up and leaned over my desk.

"Vat a tasty neck ve have here," he said. "Are you the bride of Frankenstein?" I punched Dracula in the arm, and that was the end of that.

By this time, I was getting pretty tired of the teasing, but I held up my head and tried to ignore it—until the last guy, that is. For some reason, the guy with the plastic teeth kind of got to me, and I was beginning to feel as if the whole school was against me. In fact, it was getting a little hard to keep from crying. I was having to swallow pretty hard.

Then Sam, who usually sits a couple of seats away in class, sat down in the empty desk beside me and took out his notebook and a pencil. I took a deep breath and braced myself. Sam is a reporter for the *Whistle*, our school newspaper, and I figured he wanted to do a story on my humiliation. A blow-by-blow description of the new punk culture at Willow Park High—complete with photograph.

"Hi," he said, with a grin. Sam wears glasses, and his nose is a little crooked because he ran into a truck with his bicycle once. But he does have a nice grin, if you ignore the fact that he's got a mouthful of braces. He told me once that even if he had a crooked nose, it didn't mean that he had to have crooked teeth, too.

"I'm doing a story on somebody named Maggie Mason, who used to be in this class," Sam said in a serious tone, lifting up his pencil. "She seems to have disappeared rather abruptly, and everybody's wondering what happened to her. Do you know her?"

I had to laugh. "Yeah," I said, "I think so. You mean that plain, average, sort of mousy-looking girl who used to sit at this desk?"

He brightened. "Yeah, that's the one! Except that I wouldn't exactly call her average. After all, she got an A in math from Mitchell, and if you ask me, that's pretty amazing. She's really nice, too. She's got sort of blondish hair, not mousy-looking, and—"

"Actually," I said, patting my hair, "I'm sort of partial to pink, myself."

"Pink's not bad," he said grudgingly, "but blond happens to be a favorite of mine. Anyway, this girl used to wear jeans and sort of preppy-looking sweaters a lot of the time, and she always wore this jean jacket—"

"Absolutely nondescript and blah, wouldn't you say?" I asked. I looked down at my black skirt and pink boots. "Listen, if you happen to run into this girl, tell her from me that what she needs is a complete change of wardrobe. Something a little more—"

"Shocking?" Sam suggested teasingly. There was a twinkle in his brown eyes. "Attention-getting? Something that would make a certain person sit up and take notice?"

I shifted uncomfortably. "I don't know what you're talking about." I wasn't sure why, but I really didn't want Sam to know about the crush I had on Adam. It was too embarrassing.

Sam shrugged, but the twinkle in his eyes didn't go away. "Well, anyway," he said, changing the subject, "when you see Maggie, tell her from me that I hope she's enjoying her vacation or whatever, and ask her to drop a postcard."

It was funny. Talking to Sam had made me feel a whole lot better. After that, for the rest of the day, I just smiled whenever people teased me about my outfit.

Well, things went like that all day Monday. On Tuesday, after giving the matter considerable thought, I wore my jeans tucked into the pink boots, the black top, the pink belt, and the purple vest. My hair was less spiky from sleeping on it, and the pink was beginning to fade a little.

In homeroom, I got a whole forty-five seconds from Adam. Since he was sitting there with his algebra book open, I asked him how he was doing in algebra, and he said he was doing okay if you didn't count tests. Then I asked him whether he thought the kids in Willow Park were different from the kids in L.A., and he said they were, especially in the way they dressed. I was waiting for him to say that I was more like the kids he'd known in L.A. when Jennifer showed up.

Tuesday morning was a whole lot like Monday morning as far as teasing was concerned, but it didn't bother me so much. A couple of times in the hallway, I saw Sam. He winked and grinned. I winked back. At least *one* person was on my side.

On Tuesday at lunch, I was sitting with Les and Rosita and Margot at a table in the corner of the cafeteria, talking and eating. Everybody was making a lot of noise, the way they usually do at lunchtime, laughing and telling jokes and looking around to see who was sitting with whom. Then suddenly everyone else stopped talking.

I looked up to see why. The reason was that Judd Jensen had come up to our table, and he was standing right behind me. Behind *me*! I nearly choked on my tuna salad sandwich.

I suppose every class has its tough guy. Judd Jensen is ours. He's big—big as in all muscles—and he has long black hair which he wears slicked back, with shiny stuff like grease all over it. Sometimes he wears a black leather jacket. Today he was wearing a black T-shirt with the sleeves cut off. There was a pink fluorescent skull-and-crossbones silk-screened on the front, with the words "Death Squad" under it.

"Hi, kid," he said gruffly. He pulled up a chair and sat down on it, backwards.

"Oh, uh, hi," I said, trying to swallow the piece of tuna sandwich that had gotten stuck in my throat. I took a gulp of milk. Everybody at the table had fallen silent. Les and Rosita were staring at us, and Margot had hidden her face behind her sandwich.

"Just wanted to tell you," Judd drawled, chewing on the toothpick in his mouth, "how great you're looking these days. I really dig those boots. And your hair, it's so cool." He stared at me another minute.

"Yeah," he said again, reverently, "you look like the lead singer of one of my all-time favorite bands, the Deviled Eggs."

I cleared my throat. The silence now extended to the entire cafeteria. Everybody was watching me. In the quiet, somebody crunched on a stalk of celery. I could tell that Les was going to crack up, any second.

"Uh, thank you," I said. The words came out in a sort of squeak.

"Yeah, black's my favorite color," Judd added lazily, leaning his elbows on the back of the chair. He had drawn a picture of a snake on his arm with a black ball-point pen.

"That's nice," I said feebly. Why, oh why, had I picked black?

"Listen," Judd said, his voice echoing through the silence, "I was thinking." Somebody, two or three tables away, giggled and then tried to smother it with a hiccup. But Judd didn't pay any attention.

"I was thinking that maybe you'd like to go out with me tonight. On my motorcycle." He grinned at me and put his hand on my head, touching my pink hair. "We could really have a blast, you and me, Pinky."

I pushed back my chair and stood up. When I did, the table rocked and my milk fell over, making a big puddle in the middle of the table. Rosita, who usually teases me about being a klutz, started to say something but thought better of it.

"So how about it, Pinky?" Judd asked, standing up and kicking the chair away with his foot. "Want to go for a ride?"

"Thanks a lot, Judd," I said. "But I can't go out tonight. I have something extremely urgent I have to do."

I had to wash my hair.

Chapter Six

It was harder to get the pink out of my hair than it was to put it in. But after the third shampoo, you could hardly tell that it had ever been anything but dirty blond, except for this one place over my ear that had a little pink streak. When I was done washing my hair, I hung my black outfit at the very back of the closet and put my pink boots under my bed. Then I went to sleep, and dreamed that Judd Jensen was chasing me around the cafeteria on his motorcycle. Actually, it was more like a nightmare.

It was a relief to wake up the next morning and put on my jeans and an ordinary preppy-type plaid blouse, and my old white sneakers. I considered staying home and saying that I had the stomach flu, but I decided that I'd better go back to school and face things. Besides, if I stayed home, I wouldn't get to see Adam.

"So, you're giving up?" Les asked, as we walked to school. I noticed that she was walking slower and talking to me again, now that I was back to wearing my normal, boring clothes. "On Adam DeLong, I mean."

I shook my head. "No way!" I said. I'd given the matter some very deep thought the night before, while I was washing my hair. "I'm just changing my strategy, that's all."

"But if you can't attract his attention by dressing up," Les pointed out, being logical as always, "how *do* you plan to make him notice you?"

"I haven't figured it out yet, but I will," I told her confidently. "All I need is a little time."

Les gave me a funny look. "You know," she said, "there *are* other boys in the world. There's Sam Tilden, for example. He's really a nice guy . . . and good-looking, too." There was an odd tone in her voice, but I didn't think anything of it. We always sound a little funny first thing in the morning.

"Maybe he is, but he's not *Adam*," I said. Good-looking? Sam? Sam was just Sam, and I'd never thought about whether he was good-looking or not. Anyway, I couldn't be bothered with other boys. I was remembering what my mother had said in her pep talk. What I had to do was to keep working on the Adam problem, thinking positively about how I would solve it. I'd think of a new way to capture his attention, I was sure of that.

"And of course," Les went on, "don't forget Judd Jensen, who's dying to take you out—Pinky." She giggled. "Are you going to go motorcycle riding with him tonight, or tomorrow night?"

I gritted my teeth. "I'm never going to even talk to him again," I said, glaring at her. Les got the hint and dropped the subject.

Unfortunately, nobody else at Willow Park High did. Until the end of the week, everybody I ran into at lunch called me Pinky, and a couple of kids asked me how the band was and if I had my own motorcycle yet. By the next Monday, of course, they had found somebody else to tease. They had forgotten all about me, and I was back to being just plain old Maggie. Maggie the Unremarkable.

Except for one thing, although it wasn't something that would impress Adam. We had a math test on compass angles and degrees and I got a hundred, which is practically unheard of in Mrs. Mitchell's classes. In fact, Mrs. Mitchell was so astonished by my hundred that she announced it out loud to everybody while she was handing back papers. I just sat there feeling embarrassed and blushing bright red. Even my ears were blushing. Of course, it wasn't any surprise to me. I'd really studied hard for the test. It was easy to do—I didn't exactly have to juggle my social life to fit it in or anything.

After class, Sam fell into step beside me in the hall. It was the beginning of activity period, when we were supposed to go to chorus or club meetings or study hall, if we didn't have anything else to do. I was on my way to chorus with Mr. Armbruster, and I was in a hurry. He doesn't like it if you're even ten seconds late.

"So what are you going to do to top this?" Sam asked.

"Top what?" I asked innocently, thinking of Judd's invitation. Was Sam going to tease me about him, too?

"Your hundred in math, what else?" he asked, giving me a strange look.

I breathed a sigh of relief. Maybe Sam hadn't heard about Judd and the scene in the cafeteria. "Maybe I should just get another one." I laughed. "Mrs. Mitchell would probably resign from the school if that happened."

Sam grinned. A boy dashed by, turned, and ran back toward us. "Hey, Sam!" he yelled, over the hallway noise. "I just heard the news. You've got my vote!"

"Great!" Sam said enthusiastically. "Thanks." The boy waved and ran on, narrowly missing two girls as he turned the corner.

"What news is he talking about?" I asked.

Sam shrugged. "Oh, somebody nominated me for president of the Computer Club," he said casually.

I looked at Sam with new respect. In our school, it's usually the juniors and seniors who get to be club presidents. You've got to have a whole lot going for you to get elected to anything when you're a freshman. "Hey, terrific," I said. "I'm impressed."

"Better save your applause until the votes are in," Sam said. "I'd hate for you to waste it on a nominee."

We'd gotten to my locker. I stopped to open it and about a dozen books cascaded off the top shelf and onto the floor, along with the sports bra I wear in phys ed and a very soft purple passion fruit left over from lunch a couple of days before. I snatched up the bra before Sam could see it and stuffed it back into my locker and slammed the door shut before he could get a glimpse inside. Les says my locker would win first prize in a nationwide Messy Locker Contest. Unfortunately, she's probably right.

If Sam saw the mess, he didn't make any nasty comments about it. He helped me pick up my books, and then he handed me the passion fruit with only a ghost of a smile twitching at the corners of his mouth.

"Thank you," I said, taking the passion fruit. It was very ripe, and awfully soft. I looked around for a trash can. I didn't see one. But I did see Adam, coming straight toward me. He had on this blue shirt that made his eyes look even bluer. My heart did two double back flips and settled somewhere in my throat.

For once, Adam wasn't with Jennifer. In fact, Jennifer wasn't even in sight. Maybe *this* was the time to really get his attention. I leaned sort of nonchalantly against my locker, trying to look calm and relaxed. The trouble was, I was holding this extremely ripe passion fruit, which by now was also extremely well squished and drippy in my hand. I didn't know what else I could do with it.

"Why, hello, Adam," I said, in the coolest tone I could manage.

"Uh, hi," he said, "Maggie." He looked at me. He looked at what I was holding in my hand and arched an eyebrow. "Dessert?" he asked.

I blushed. "It . . . it's a—" I gulped. "It's a passion fruit." I gave him what I hoped was a suggestive glance. "I'm a very passionate person."

Adam looked at me. Then he just shook his head and turned and walked away, into the computer room down the hall.

Very quietly, I put the passion fruit back into my locker and closed the door. Then I tore a piece of paper out of my notebook and tried to wipe the goop and juice off my hand.

Sam turned to look at Adam's back disappearing into the computer room, and then he looked at me. "Is it possible," he said thoughtfully, "that Adam DeLong doesn't recognize a passion fruit when he sees one?"

I couldn't help it. In spite of myself, I had to giggle.

"Oh, by the way," he added casually, glancing at my hair. "If you see that girl with the pink hair who was hanging around here last week, tell her from me that she looks a lot better these days."

"Thanks," I said. "I will."

If the conversation with Sam was an upper, there were so many downers in my life that it sort of got lost in the shuffle. It wasn't only Adam. It was my family again. My dearly beloved, wonderfully remarkable family.

It was the same night that I got the hundred in math. Given the way I was feeling—about Adam, I mean, and all the money I'd spent, only to attract the attention of a certain member of the local motorcycle gang—I was really looking forward to having something good to talk about at dinner for once. My hundred certainly qualified.

This time, I had decided not to spoil the effect of my big announcement by telling one person at a time. I was going to save my news and tell everybody all at once, while we were eating dinner and I could get everybody's attention. It was a good night for announcing something important like that, because everybody was home, for a change.

But it turned out that it wasn't such a great night for making a big announcement about my test grade. Or maybe it was a good night, but my timing was off. Anyway, we'd just sat down at the table and Dad had started to dish up the lasagne, and I opened my mouth to tell everybody the good news.

"Guess what, everybody," I announced, looking around. "We had a math test at school and I—"

"Excuse me, Maggie," my mother said, interrupting. She frowned at Frog. "Frog, did you wash your hands before you came to the table?"

Frog spread out his hands and examined them. "No," he said. "But they're clean—I just got out of the pool."

"Young man," my father said, in the tone he uses to warn us that we're almost in trouble.

"Yes, sir," Frog said. He stood up. "But before I go, can I tell you something?"

"Wait," I said, "I already—"

"But I have to wash my hands," Frog told me in a pained voice. He looked around at everybody and then puffed out his chest. "They announced the swimming team for the district meet today. I'm on it," he said.

"Oh, Frog!" my mother exclaimed, "that's wonderful!"

"Terrific, son." My father beamed a huge smile at Frog. He seemed to have forgotten all about Frog's bad manners.

"That's great, Froggie," Ellyn said.

"Yeah, great," I said.

Frog looked at Mom. "Do I still have to wash my hands?"

Mom nodded. Heaving a heavy sigh, Frog turned and stomped out of the room. For somebody who loves the water, he certainly hates to wash in it.

I stared after Frog. Maybe it would be a good idea to wait until he got back, I thought. I took a plate of lasagne from my dad and began to eat.

Next to me, Ellyn sat forward on her chair. "Listen, everybody," she said enthusiastically, "I have this terrific news that I just can't wait to tell you!"

"Oh, really?" Dad asked. He handed her a plate of lasagne. "What is it?"

"It's *wonderful*," Ellyn went on. "It's the greatest thing that could happen to me."

"Well, you'd better hurry up and tell us what it is," Dad remarked. "You look like a balloon about to pop."

My mother smiled gently at him. "Now, Howard," she said, "don't tease the children."

Ellyn looked chagrined. "I'm not a child," she said.

"Of course you're not, dear," my mother murmured. "Tell us your news."

"It's about the yearbook," Ellyn said, sounding important.

"Now, wait a minute," I objected. If Ellyn was going to tell us something about the yearbook, I had the feeling that I'd better get my news in ahead of her. "I was about to tell—"

Frog came back into the room and sat down. He held up his hands in front of his face. "See?" he said triumphantly. "All clean."

"Listen, it's *my* turn, Ellyn," I protested. "I wanted to tell everybody about—"

My mother put her hand on my arm. "In a minute, Maggie," she said. She leaned forward. "Now what about the yearbook, Ellyn?"

Ellyn looked around the table. "The results of the yearbook election were announced today," she said, and paused dramatically.

My father put down his fork. "And how did it turn out?" he asked, with interest.

Ellyn waited another five seconds while everybody looked at her. Then, as if she couldn't hold it back any longer, she said, "I won! I was elected yearbook editor!"

My mother got up and came around the table and hugged Ellyn. "That is wonderful, dear!" she said mistily. "You know, I was yearbook editor when I was in high school. It's an experience I've never forgotten."

My father raised his glass of milk. "Let's have a toast," he proposed, "to Miss Ellyn Mason, Editor-of-the-Year!"

Frog lifted his glass and banged it against my father's. "I'll drink to that," he said.

"Me, too," I said, with a resigned sigh.

When everybody had finished drinking their toast to Ellyn, Mom turned to me. "Now, did you say you had something to tell us, dear?" she asked.

I looked around. Everybody was busy eating lasagne.

"Yes," I said. "I got a hundred today! On my math test. On compass angles. You know, Mrs. Mitchell is one of the hardest teachers at school, too."

"That's nice, Maggie," my mother said, patting my arm. "We're proud of you. It isn't everybody who can get such good grades in math." She looked around the table. "Who would like some more salad?"

"Never can tell when we'll need a mathematician to help us figure out compass angles," my father said heartily. "Or maybe you could help me balance the checkbook." He frowned at Frog. "Frog, would your elbows be offended if we asked them to leave the table?"

"That's great, Margaret," Ellyn said. "I wish I could do math as easily as you do." She pushed her chair back and looked around the table. "Would anybody mind if I excused myself? I want to call Laura and tell her the news about the yearbook, in case she hasn't heard."

"Fine, but don't forget the dishes, dear," my mother reminded her. "It's your turn."

Frog moved his elbows off the table. "So, are there seconds on lasagne for the next district champion?" he asked hopefully.

I dragged myself slowly up the stairs. By the time I'd finally been able to make my big announcement, it hadn't been so big anymore—relatively speaking, that is. I'd been upstaged by a swim meet and the yearbook election. Not even the fact that it was Ellyn's night to do the dishes could make me feel better.

I went into our bedroom. Dejectedly, I turned on the television set on our dresser and flopped down on my bed to watch a sit-com, the very last thing I wanted to do. Over in the corner, Doodle was asleep on top of my pink sweatshirt, making squeaky little yelps while his tail thumped the floor, as if he was having a dream about chasing a cat.

The sit-com was even worse than usual. It was about this spacy girl who was trying to impress her boss by showing him how much she knew about computers. When it was over, I turned off the TV and lay back on the bed, staring at the ceiling and thinking. But I could only think about two things. About what a great big bomb my great big announcement had turned out to be. And how rejected I had felt when Adam turned his back, walked away, and went into the computer room.

After a few minutes my thoughts began to get hazy—the way they do when you're about halfway between dreaming and being awake—and I began to imagine how that incident at my locker with Adam could have been different. In my halfway dream I didn't just stand there, gawking after Adam like some sort of lovesick junior high student. No, I was walking *with* him, hand in hand, into the computer room.

"Actually, Maggie," Adam was telling me in a reassuring tone, "it's not at all difficult to work on a computer. All you have to do is remember a few basic commands." He smiled gently down at me. "If you have time, I'd love to give you a private lesson."

His smile melted my insides like butter. "Of course," I said. "That would be totally wonderful."

And then the two of us sat down at the computer, very close together, and Adam began to give me a lesson. Then he turned the computer over to me. And that's when I really amazed him.

"Oh, is *that* all there is to it?" I asked airily. "Why, I thought it was supposed to be hard."

My fingers flying like a virtuoso pianist, I began to enter this extremely complicated program. Adam just sat there, watching, stunned by my skill. When I had finished and hit the Save key, he broke into wild applause.

"That's amazing, Maggie," he said. "You're incredible! I can't believe I never noticed you before. I feel like the luckiest guy in the world."

Then suddenly my family was there, with Les and Sam, and they began to applaud, too. Everyone was shouting "Encore, encore!" I got up to take a little bow, and Adam handed me a dozen beautiful red roses and kissed me on the cheek. I was sniffling, the way girls do when they've just been named Miss America or something like that.

Out in the hall, the phone rang. I sat up straight, and my dream ended just as if somebody had turned off the projector. But it didn't matter, because I'd had a great idea. I knew how I was going to get Adam DeLong to notice me!

Frog knocked at the door. "It's for you," he said. "It's you-know-who. You know, the only person who ever calls you?"

I jumped up and ran to the phone. "I've got it, Les!" I cried, excited. "I've got it!"

"Hello?" Les said. "Got what? Not another outfit, I hope."

"No, no, I've got it all figured out, that's what. How I'm going to get Adam's attention." I thought of the roses and the kiss on the cheek. "And this time it's foolproof," I added. "It absolutely, positively *cannot* fail."

"Who says?" Les asked.

"*I* say, that's who," I retorted hotly. "Leslie Langsdorf, just for once I wish you'd stop throwing cold water over my good ideas—especially before you even hear what they are." Which wasn't very fair, actually, because Les usually supports my ideas, even when she isn't wildly enthusiastic about them.

"Okay, okay, I'm sorry," Les said. "Please tell me your great idea, Maggie."

"Adam is into computers," I said. "I saw him going into the computer room this afternoon."

"So?"

"So I'm going to get him to teach me how to run the computer," I replied. "Isn't that a great idea?" I gave a dreamy sigh. "There we'll be, sitting side by side, our hands on the same keyboard, our knees touching, the air full of the electricity of our nearness—" I giggled. "A hands-on session, so to speak. Well, what do you think?"

There was a pause on the other end of the line, and then a munching sound. I suspected that Les was eating potato chips. "But you already know how to work on the computer, don't you, Maggie? I mean, you had a computer course back in junior high, didn't you?" Les asked.

"Sure," I said, grinning. It was true. I'd taken the course; in fact, Sam had been in it with me—and I'd gotten an A. But Adam didn't know that. Anyway, it was all part of my plan. "Sure, I know how to use it. That's the best part."

"Oh, now I get it," Les said, the light beginning to dawn. "You're going to pretend to Adam that you don't know anything about computers, and then when he shows you, you're going to impress him with how quickly you can learn. He'll be so bowled over by your ability that he'll fall at your feet. Right?"

"Right," I said. "Well?"

"Well," Les replied slowly, "apart from the minor consideration that it's unethical, dishonest, and just slightly crazy, I suppose it might work."

"Listen," I said, between my teeth, "I'm to the point where a little dishonesty is acceptable, as long as it does the job. Anyway, you know what they say. 'All's fair in love and war.'"

"Tsk, tsk," Les said. She paused. "Listen, Maggie, speaking of war . . . how would you like to come over tonight and help me baby-sit the Royal Pain? My sister just brought him over, and my mother has suddenly remembered a huge department store sale she has to go to for the next three hours."

I shuddered. "If it's all the same to you,

Les, I think I'll skip it tonight. I'm not really in the mood for baby-sitting." I wanted to take a nice warm bubble bath, paint my toenails, and think more dreamy thoughts about Adam—and my new idea, Plan B.

Les sighed. "Don't say I didn't give you your chance," she said.

Chapter Seven

I'd learned my lesson. I wasn't going to rush into this scheme the way I'd rushed into the other one, without thinking through all the possible consequences. So I thought about it as carefully as I could, examining the idea from every angle. Try as I might, I couldn't think of anything that could possibly go wrong with it. But the timing was going to be very important. I had to pick exactly the right moment; Adam had to be alone in the computer room, and there had to be plenty of time before the bell rang to end activity period.

That meant I had to watch the room and make my move when Adam went in. The fact that my locker was just down the hall from the computer room made things a little easier. At least that gave me a legitimate reason—in Adam's eyes, anyway, I hoped—to be hanging out in the hallway. The trouble was that the teachers' lounge was across the hall. Which meant that some nosy teacher might want to know why I was hanging out in front of my locker during activity period, when I was supposed to be somewhere doing something constructive—like singing scales for Mr. Armbruster. But I was willing to take the chance.

So the first day, I waited. After the bell rang, I stood in front of my locker nonchalantly, my arms full of books, trying to look as if I had just that second come along, and in another second or two, I was going to be on my way someplace else—all the while keeping one eye on the computer room door. It was kind of hard, because people kept going by and giving me funny looks.

Then Sam went by, and stopped.

"Hi, Maggie," he said. He smiled at me. He looked different somehow, but I wasn't quite sure why.

"Uh, hi," I said.

He gave me a curious look. "Are you waiting for somebody?"

"No. No, I'm not waiting for anybody. Not at all." I shifted my books from one arm to another.

He gave me another look. "Well, then, why are you standing here?"

"I'm not waiting for anybody, *exactly,*" I

said nervously. I didn't want Sam to know that I was waiting to make a move on Adam—even though I had the sneaking suspicion that he already knew that. I lowered my voice to a whisper. "I . . . I'm taking a poll," I lied.

Sam grinned. "I see," he said. He looked over his shoulder, in the direction of the computer room, then leaned closer. "But why are we whispering?" he whispered.

I looked at him. "Because it's a confidential poll," I said. I felt a little tingle go up my spine. I couldn't remember ever being this close to Sam before, and for some reason, it made me feel kind of funny.

Sam looked up and down the hallway, and then leaned close again. "Let me guess," he whispered. His breath tickled my ear. "You're counting the number of kids on skateboards."

I shook my head, smiling a little.

"Rollerskates?"

"Not quite," I said with a giggle.

Sam stepped back and snapped his fingers. "I've got it," he said. "You're working undercover for the principal. You've staked out the teachers' lounge, and you're clocking the number of minutes each teacher spends drinking coffee."

"How did you guess?" I asked, shaking

my head in pretended amazement. "You've completely blown my cover."

Sam laughed. "How could I miss it? You're so transparent, Maggie."

"Yeah." I shifted my books again. "Transparent. That's me."

Sam touched my arm. "Well, let me know if you need somebody to stake out the parking lot," he said with a grin, and walked away.

Just then I figured out what was different about Sam. His braces were gone, and you could see his teeth when he smiled, instead of a mouthful of silver wires. It was a nice difference, and I was beginning to like talking to Sam, more than almost anybody else I knew. Still, I was glad he was gone. In my dream, it had seemed very logical to have an audience for my computer lesson with Adam. But not in real life. Especially not an audience who knew that I'd already gotten an A in computers—and who had already sort of suggested that I had a major crush on Adam. I was beginning to be afraid I was transparent in more ways than one. Adam looked right past me, and Sam seemed to see right through me.

The minutes ticked by, and there was no sign of Adam. After a while I began to feel very conspicuous. hanging out in a half-empty hallway when everybody else was on their way somewhere. So I gave it up and went to chorus, with the idea of sneaking in by the back door while everybody was up on the risers, so that Mr. Armbruster wouldn't see that I was late. It would have worked, too, if Hallie Hanson (who stands in front of me) had been just six inches taller. As it was, Mr. Armbruster saw me walk in, and he gave a ten-minute lecture on "the importance of arriving on time for one's engagements," as he put it. The whole chorus was mad at me. Why couldn't I be invisible when I was late to class? I wondered.

The next time we had activity period, I was prepared. No more hanging out in the hallway, trying to look like I was on my way somewhere. This time I was going to have something to do—something that would keep me at my locker for the entire period, if necessary. It was easier today, because chorus had been canceled and I was supposed to be in study hall. I told Miss Ashlock, the study hall teacher, what I had to do. She agreed that it was pretty important and that I ought to get on it right away before the situation got out of hand.

The something I was going to do while I waited for Adam was to clean out my locker. I mean, this was a really legitimate thing to do, because my locker had gone from bad to worse in a very short time. I was afraid that if I didn't take matters in hand pretty soon, they might get *out* of hand. Les knew somebody once who got roaches in her locker and had to use roach repellant to get rid of them. Everybody knew about it because her gym suit always smelled like chemicals, even when it was clean.

So that's why I was standing in the hall, carefully positioned so that I could keep an eye on the door of the computer room. I was pulling a stack of books and papers off the top shelf, trying to keep them from sliding onto the floor, when somebody came up behind me.

"Hi," he said, in a gravelly voice. "Say, Pinky, what'd you do to your hair? I really dug you the old way."

It was Judd Jensen.

That's when it happened. I was so startled by Judd's unexpected appearance that I dropped my arms. The books and papers cascaded out of my locker and onto the floor, and with them the large can of pink spray-on hair coloring that was left over from my attempt to change my image. I'd put it in my locker, planning to use it to keep my hair looking fresh and pink throughout the day. What a mistake. The spray can lost its lid, bounced upside down, then landed right side up, on top of my dictionary on the floor. The pink dye began to spray with this evil-sounding hiss, like one of those bug foggers you see advertised on television. I gulped and put my hands over my eyes. Could things get any worse?

Judd looked at the pink fog, looked at me standing there peering through my hands, and took three steps backward. Then he turned and practically sprinted in the other direction. By this time, half a dozen other kids had gathered in the hallway, watching from a safe distance while the can continued to spit out a pink cloud.

"What do you think it is?" one guy asked another. "A bomb?"

A girl giggled. "Does it have an off switch?" she asked. Somebody snickered, and in a minute the whole crowd was laughing. I just stood there, feeling horribly klutzy and miserably embarrassed and wishing with all my heart that I was at home with the flu.

"Maggie?" Sam suddenly stepped out from the crowd. "What's going on?"

"Sam, can you please make it stop?" I pleaded.

Sam ducked around the can to keep from getting sprayed pink, reached down and quickly took care of it. The can stopped hissing, and the pink cloud slowly began to thin out.

"Here you are," Sam said casually, picking up the can and handing it to me.

"Uh, thanks," I said. "How did you do it?" I looked at the can, feeling humiliated. It was bad enough that it had gone off. That it had gone off with such a huge pink cloud, right in the middle of the hall, was awful. On top of that, it would remind everyone of my disastrous days as "Pinky," Judd's girl. I wanted to put a paper bag on my head.

"Aerosols have a little valve on them," Sam explained in a matter-of-fact way, as if turning off runaway aerosols was something he did two or three times a day. "This one got bent when it fell—that's what made it go off. All I did was straighten it out."

I shook my head. "I don't know how to thank you," I mumbled. I meant it. How could I thank him for rescuing me from becoming a school joke? Suddenly, on impulse, I stood on my tiptoes and kissed his cheek. Then, blushing furiously, I backed away. Why had I done that?

It was at that moment that I saw Adam disappearing into the computer room.

Chapter Eight

"Uh, excuse me, Sam," I said. I began to scoop up my books and notebooks—my dictionary was now pink—and toss them back into my locker. Cleaning out my locker was going to have to wait for another day. "I've got to go."

Sam turned to look in the direction of the computer room. "Well, see you later," he said, and turned and walked away.

I straightened up and looked in the mirror that was taped to my locker door. I ran a comb through my hair, tucking the pinkish strands behind my ears, and dabbed on a bit of lip gloss. Then I closed the door, took a deep breath, and walked down the hall to the computer room, praying that it would be empty—except for Adam, of course.

It was.

Rumor had it that the computer room had once been a broom closet. It wasn't very big—just room enough for a table on one side and two computer stations on the other. One of them had an Out of Order sign on it. Adam was sitting in front of the other one, his back to the door.

"Why, hello, Adam," I said, as if I were surprised to find him there. If I sounded breathless, it was because I was. After all, it was the first time Adam and I had ever been alone together. My heart was pounding, and my pulse was racing. I hoped I wouldn't faint on the spot—or if I did, that at least I would do it gracefully.

Adam was working on a disk and the monitor screen was filled with columns of little green numbers, it looked like. At the sound of my voice, he swiveled around and looked at me.

"Oh, yeah. Hi, Maggie," he said. He swiveled back around again as if he wished I'd go away. But I wasn't going to be brushed aside. I mean, this was my big chance—the one I'd been waiting for.

"What a lucky break to find you here," I said, coming into the room.

"Oh, yeah?" he asked, sounding mildly interested. He added another row of numbers. "How come?"

I pulled out the chair next to his and sat down. It was one of those chairs that have wheels, and it rolled easily across the waxed tile floor.

"Because I've been thinking for a long time that it would be really great to learn how to operate one of these things," I said, gesturing at the computer. "Wow, just look at all those keys, you must have to be a genius to figure out how to use them all!" I leaned closer, getting a wonderful whiff of something spicy—aftershave, maybe?

Of course, I wasn't really impressed by the computer. I knew what all those buttons and lights and keys and things did. I also knew that the whole system was so simple to operate that even Frog could use it. But Adam didn't know that I knew that. He didn't know anything about me—that was the problem.

"Well, no, it's not really hard to learn," he said modestly. "This particular computer is supposed to be one of the more user-friendly models." Still, his tone implied that I had been right the first time and that you really did have to know a lot to be able to figure it out.

"User-friendly." I laughed lightly. "That's cute." There was only one user I wanted to be friendly with. I rolled my chair a little closer to his. "What're all those numbers up on the screen?" I asked.

"Oh, that's a program I've been working on for the last couple of weeks," Adam said proudly. "It's designed to random-match two separate populations. See?" He hit a key and the two columns on the monitor jiggled and then realigned themselves. "What it does is match up one name from Column A with another name from Column B."

I wasn't interested in random-matching from Column A and Column B. What I was interested in was matching on purpose, as in matching Adam and Maggie. But I couldn't exactly tell Adam that.

"That's fascinating," I observed aloud. I stared at the keyboard for a minute. "Do you suppose," I asked hesitantly, "that you could show me a few of the fundamentals?" Fundamentals like hugging and kissing were what I had in mind, but they were way in the future, after I'd gotten used to just sitting beside Adam. If he kissed me right now I would probably fall off my chair.

Adam glanced at his watch. "I don't really think I have time today, Maggie," he began. "I need to finish this program, and then I have to—"

"Oh, it would only take a few minutes," I wheedled. "I mean, you don't have to show me anything fancy. Just a few simple commands, that's all. Then another time we could get into the more complicated stuff." You see, I was laying the groundwork for another computer date with him.

"Well, I guess," Adam said reluctantly. He rolled his chair back and stood up. "You sit here."

As I got up to sit in Adam's chair, my hand brushed against his. My fingers tingled from his touch, and there were goose bumps on the back of my neck. I had been right. There was electricity between us. I could only hope that Adam felt it, too.

"If we're going to do this," Adam said, "let's get started. I don't have all day." He was standing right behind my chair—very close.

I nodded. I wished he'd be a little nicer, but that would probably come later, when we were better acquainted. Anyway, I'd always heard that men have a hard time expressing their deeper, more tender feelings. Maybe that was Adam's problem.

"So what do I do now?" I asked, staring at the keyboard. I gave a helpless-sounding little giggle. "It's all so confusing."

"Well, first," Adam said in a take-charge

voice, "we want to save what's already on the screen. There's some new stuff there that I don't want to lose."

I raised my hands over the keyboard. "Save," I murmured. "How do I do that?"

Adam leaned over me. I could feel his breath on my neck, and I broke out in a cold sweat. It was getting hard to breathe.

He pointed. "See that key—the one with the little apple on it? You hit that key with one hand and the S key with the other. Doing that saves everything that's in the file."

I looked. "Oh, yes," I said. "Well, that doesn't look so hard."

I hit the keys. All of a sudden, all the figures and columns on the screen disappeared.

"Oh, *no*!" Adam groaned. "You idiot! You hit the D instead of the S! You just deleted my whole file!"

"I did?"

I stared at the keyboard. I couldn't believe I had done such a stupid thing. I'd never done it before, even when I was learning the computer the first time. The only way I could explain it was the nervousness from having Adam so close to me, breathing on my neck and touching my hand. But I couldn't exactly tell him that was why I'd messed up.

Adam was holding his head. "I can't believe it," he moaned. "All that work—gone!"

"But I don't understand," I said. "Don't you have it stored on the disk?" I stood up and opened the disk drive and pulled out the disk. "Isn't this it? The disk, I mean?"

"Yes, but I made some really important changes just before you got here, and I hadn't saved them yet. Now I've got to figure out those changes all over again—and all because *you* zapped them into electronic oblivion."

"Oh, Adam, I'm really sorry," I said. Actually, I was more than sorry, I was miserable. This wasn't going at all the way it had in my dream.

"Well, it's too late for sorry." Adam reached for the disk. "Listen, you'd better give me that disk before something happens to it. I don't have a backup." He took the disk out of my hand and sort of pushed me aside, rolling the chair sideways with his foot.

I don't know exactly what happened next. I think that Adam dropped the disk on the floor. Anyway, I bent over to pick it up just as the chair rolled over it. At that moment Adam reached for the disk, too. He bumped into me and I felt myself falling. I didn't want to knock over the table, so I grabbed for something to steady myself. Unfortunately, what I grabbed was the power cord to the monitor. I sat down hard on the floor and the monitor toppled over with an enormous *crash*!

"Oh, *no*!" Adam moaned again.

I tried to get up.

"Just stay there," Adam said grimly, putting his hand on my head and holding me down. "That way, maybe you won't knock over anything else." He bent over and picked up the crushed disk and stood there looking back and forth between the disk and the monitor, lying on its side.

I swallowed. My face was burning and I felt like crying. I couldn't believe I had been such a klutz. Never in my life had I been so uncoordinated—and now, when it mattered most, I'd looked like a *complete* fool.

"Is it broken?" I asked, pointing to the monitor.

"I don't know." Adam turned it right side up, plugged it in, and flicked the switch. But the screen didn't light up. We waited a minute or two. Nothing happened.

He turned around to me. "Yeah, it's broken," he said. "And my disk is totally trashed," he added bitterly, "and with no backup, I'll have to start over from scratch."

I struggled to my feet and set the chair upright. I could tell that my face was bright red from embarrassment, but I had to try to at least say something to salvage my pride.

"Well," I said, trying to be cheerful, "you can use the other computer to rewrite your program, can't you?"

"Sure, if it was working," he said, gesturing toward the Out of Order sign. "It takes weeks to get these things repaired, you know." He sighed. "This means that I'll never get this program finished in time for the orienteering meet."

I had no idea what orienteering was, but I could tell from the look on Adam's face that I hadn't exactly made a big hit with him.

"Oh, Adam," I said, blinking back the tears, "I wish I could tell you how sorry I am about this. I—"

At that moment the door opened. It was Sam. He looked a little flustered when he saw us—or me, with my eyes all watery and my face all red.

"Sorry," Sam muttered, "I didn't mean to interrupt. I just came to see if they got the cable fixed on the monitor yet."

Adam's head jerked up. "The cable?"

"Yeah—on that monitor you're working with. It was loose or something yesterday."

"Well, the monitor's out now," Adam said disgustedly. He threw me a look. "I was showing Maggie here how to run the computer, and she managed to wipe out my file, trash my disk, and destroy the monitor and—"

"*You* were showing Maggie how to use it?" Sam asked, not bothering to hide his surprise. "But she already knows how—" He stopped and looked at me. Then he nodded and a teasing twinkle came into his eyes. "I see," he said.

I was afraid he did.

"Here, let me have a look at the monitor," Sam said, stepping forward. He reached behind it and jiggled something. Suddenly, the screen began to glow. "There," he said.

"You mean, it's fixed?" I asked.

Sam nodded. "There's this loose cable in the back," he said. "You have to wiggle it a couple of times to get it to work."

"Thanks," Adam said grudgingly. "I didn't know that."

Sam turned to me and raised his eyebrows. "Listen, Maggie," he said, beginning to smile, "any time you want a lesson on the computer, just let me know. I'd be glad to show you the basics. You know, the kind of stuff they taught us back in junior high, when we had that course on—"

"Yeah, great," I said. I couldn't stand being humiliated any longer. I picked up my books and ran out.

I was so humiliated that I didn't wait for Les after school, the way I usually do. I just walked home, feeling dismal and sad and wishing that I could disappear for a few weeks or move to another town or something. I'd wanted to make Adam notice me—and he had. Now, he would never, ever forget what a total and complete klutz I was. I had thought my scheme was foolproof, but I'd blown it. Absolutely *blown* it. And then there was the business with the spray can in the hallway in front of half the freshman class. I felt utterly, totally mortified.

The phone rang when I was coming in the door. It was Les.

"Hey, what happened to you?" she asked. "I waited, but you didn't show up in front after school."

"Listen," I said dejectedly, "I don't really feel like talking just now. Can I call you back later?"

"But I've got something to tell you," Les said. "Something you'll really be—"

"Later, okay, Les?" I sighed. "I just can't talk now," I explained and hung up.

Dinner that night was as fun and excit ing as always—for everybody but me, that is. Frog announced that his swim team was going to be interviewed on television. Ellyn told us that she had been picked to be in a juniors' fashion show featuring local high school students at the mall. My mother said that she and my father were going to be featured in the LifeStyle section of the Orlando newspaper. Then everybody turned to look at me, as if they expected me to be a news item, too.

"How was your day today, Maggie?" my mother chirped brightly.

I stabbed my spinach salad with a fork and looked down. "Miserable," I muttered.

"Oh, come now, you don't mean that," my father said. "Here, have another piece of chicken. That'll make you feel better."

Barbequed chicken is high on my list of favorite things to eat.

"Yes, I do too mean it," I said. Nothing, not even barbequed chicken, was going to make me feel better. I pushed back my plate. "I don't feel like eating tonight. May I be excused?"

My mother looked a little worried. She leaned forward and put her hand on my forehead. "Are you sick?" she asked.

"No," I said, and stood up.

But I was sick. I felt like I was going to die whenever I thought of the disgusted look on Adam's face in the computer room. I had wanted to impress him with my cleverness, and all I'd done was make an idiot out of myself. "Excuse me," I said.

I ran up the stairs to my room and flung myself across the bed. There was a startled yelp. Doodle must be under the bed, I thought. I leaned over and pulled up a corner of the spread. Yep, Doodle was under the bed, all right. I stared at him for a minute and then closed my eyes.

He was chewing one of my pink boots.

Chapter Nine

"Doodle ate your boot?" Les asked unbelievingly.

I nodded into the phone. "He chewed off the heel. I guess he liked the way it smelled. Or maybe he just likes pink. Or maybe he doesn't like pink, and this was his way of showing it."

Les sighed. "Too bad. Once I got used to them, the boots were the best part of your outfit."

"Maybe I ought to get a new heel."

"Maybe you ought to get a new dog."

"Unfortunately," I reminded her, "Doodle isn't *my* dog. He's Frog's dog."

"Let him eat Frog's boots, then," Les said helpfully. "Or his flippers, or whatever. Anyway, I didn't call about Doodle."

"So what did you call about?" I asked.

"Don't be so grumpy," Les told me. "I called with an idea about Adam. You're always saying that I throw cold water on your ideas, but here's one for you, free of charge. About how you can get him to notice you, that is."

"It's too late," I said glumly. "He's noticed me already. He'll never forget me, as long as he lives."

"Oh, really? That's great! How did you manage that?"

"No, it *isn't* great," I sighed. "And it wasn't easy, either." I told her about the way I'd disgraced myself in the computer room, which took awhile. After that I told her what had happened with the spray can, and how Sam had come along and turned it off. Telling all this took about fifteen minutes. Les didn't interrupt once.

"You did all *that*?" Les asked, in an awed voice, when I had finished with my story. "In just one afternoon?"

"Yeah. Sad, but true. Maybe I should have let you throw cold water on my idea in the first place. Adam's got to think I'm the biggest loser in the freshman class. And I wouldn't be surprised if Sam did, too."

Les sighed. "I doubt that. Well, Maggie, here's what you have to do. You have to put that behind you. It's in the past and you can't do anything about it. What you have to do is focus on the future," she chirped.

"Les," I said, "you've been watching too many sappy movies."

"I have not!" she protested. "I made that up all on my own. Okay, now on to Plan C. Did you know that Adam's organizing something called an orienteering club?"

"Yeah," I growled. "That was what was on the disk I trashed. Some data he was random-matching for orienteering—whatever that is. I've never heard of it."

"Well, *I* know what orienteering is," Les said smugly. "It's a new school club that Adam's organizing, because he was in one back in California. Mr. Cowper told me about it. He's going to be the faculty advisor for the club." Mr. Cowper is the boys' phys ed instructor. He's my homeroom teacher, too.

"So what is it?" I asked.

"It's a wilderness sport. Sort of like playing hide-and-seek out in the woods, except that you use a compass to follow a map that shows you what the course is. The person who gets around the course first wins."

"Hmmmm," I said. I was beginning to see what Les was driving at.

"Now," Les said, "didn't you get the Finding Your Way badge in Girl Scouts? The same month you got your Ecology badge?"

"Yeah." It was one of the few remarkable things I'd ever done, getting two badges in one month. "But that was an awfully long time ago," I added doubtfully. "Two or three years ago." Still, it sounded like the same thing, following maps and using a compass to find your way around, stuff like that.

"It's probably like riding a bike or playing a piano," Les assured me. "Some things you never forget. So what do you think?"

"I think," I said slowly, "that you might have something there." I paused. "Are you going to join the club? I mean, I'd feel a lot better about it if I had somebody to do it with me. Then if I get lost, I won't get lost alone."

"Who, me?" Les said, horrified. "Me—go out into the jungle? You know better than that, Maggie. I mean, if a snake even looked at me, I'd die of fright. And I hate swamps, with all that yukky Spanish moss and those ferocious crocodiles and—"

"Alligators," I corrected her. "Crocodiles live in Africa, when they're not hanging out at the zoo." I didn't get my Ecology badge for nothing. "But I thought you said this was going to be in the woods," I pointed out, "not the jungle."

"Yes, but there aren't any woods around here, remember? This is Florida. Anything that isn't a parking lot or a mall is a swamp."

I remembered all too well. In the Girl Scouts, they had taken us to the Ocala National Forest so we could prove how well we could use a compass and follow a map that took us in big circles through the forest. Except that the forest was really a jungle, with sharp-pointed palmetto palms and slash pines and vines and creepy Spanish moss that dripped down from the trees. It was an experience I'd never forget—and one that I wasn't crazy about repeating. Nevertheless, I *was* crazy about Adam. I would happily follow him anywhere, even to the ends of the earth. Even into a swamp of mosquitoes and palmetto.

"Let's see if I've got this straight," I said. "Your idea is that I'll join the Orienteering Club and impress Adam by showing him how well I can follow a map through the untracked wilderness. Is that pretty much it?"

"You got it," Less said happily. "Isn't it a fabulous idea?"

"And while I'm out swatting mosquitoes and falling into holes and admiring alligators, you'll be at home with a tall glass of iced tea and some dip and chips, filing your nails and watching soap operas. Right?"

"Right again." Les laughed cheerfully. "Well, what do you think? Don't you agree that Adam will have to be impressed when you take first place at the orienteering meet?"

"I guess," I said, remembering the look on Adam's face when he saw his destroyed disk. "Anyway, I'm willing to give it a try."

If you want to know the truth, I was ready to give up on making a good impression on Adam. After what had happened, it was more a matter of redeeming myself, and getting rid of the horrible first impression I'd made that afternoon. But I didn't want to tell Les that.

"Good," Les said smugly. "I'm glad I went ahead and signed you up, then."

"What?" I squawked. "You signed me up? Without even asking?"

"I just asked, didn't I? Anyway, I figured this was one idea you'd really be excited about."

"Yeah," I said glumly. "I'm just *dying* to get out in the swamp again."

"Listen, Maggie," Les said, ignoring my last comment, "about Sam . . ." Her voice trailed off.

"Well?" I asked. "What about Sam?"

Les cleared her throat. "I was just wondering if you'd noticed that he got his braces off a few days ago."

I thought of Sam's nice smile, and the teasing twinkle in his eyes when he had walked in on the disaster in the computer room. "Yes," I said. "I noticed."

There was a minute of silence. "Don't you think," Les asked finally, "that he looks really cute? Now that you can see his teeth, I mean."

"Yes," I said, "I do." Was Les getting interested in Sam? After we hung up, I sat and thought about this unexpected turn of events for a few minutes. I wasn't exactly sure how I felt about it.

"Maggie, are you absolutely *sure* you want to do this?"

I looked up from my history homework and blinked. It was Adam, and he was talking to me. He was actually, voluntarily talking to *me*—in homeroom, no less, in front of twenty other people.

I took a deep breath to steady my nerves. "Do what?" I asked, in almost my normal voice. He was wearing a dark blue shirt, a couple of shades deeper than his eyes, and a pair of neatly presed khaki cords. Just looking at him was enough to make my day—and he was *talking* to me! Maybe he hadn't been as angry at me as I thought.

Adam held out a piece of paper. At the top, it said Orienteering Club, and underneath that was a list of about thirty names. My name was on the list—in Les's handwriting.

"Are you sure orienteering is really your kind of sport?" he asked, implying that he was pretty sure it wasn't.

"Well, yes," I said, ignoring his snobby tone, "as a matter of fact, I think it is my kind of sport. And it sounds like a lot of fun."

"But are you sure you know what you're getting into?" Adam persisted. He sat down in the empty seat just in front of mine. "I mean, in orienteering we don't just play around. This is really survival stuff. You've got to be tough and have plenty of endurance. We climb mountains—"

"But there aren't any mountains to climb around here," I pointed out. "This is Florida, not California. What we have in Florida are beaches and swamps. I don't suppose there's any chance," I added hopefully, "that we might be doing this orienteering stuff on a beach?"

Adam shook his head. "It's a wilderness activity," he said, as if *wilderness* were a foreign word and he had to say it slowly for me. "It's a test of your ability to make your way through woods and forests, really dense forests, full of wild animals and"—he looked at me—"snakes. There are bound to be snakes."

"Well, I've got my Finding Your Way badge," I told him, "from the Girl Scouts. We learned how to use a compass and how to read a map. And I'm not afraid of snakes."

Adam gave me a scornful look. "Girl Scouts," he said, with the same pitying tone that he might have used to say "Sunday school picnic."

For a minute I was almost angry, but then he brushed the dark hair out of his eyes, and I stopped being angry and just wanted to melt. Adam could be as scornful of the Girl Scouts as he wanted to be, as far as I was concerned, as long as he kept on being so nice to look at.

"Listen, Adam, I'll try my best," I said meekly. "My *very* best."

Adam sighed. I hoped he wasn't thinking that my best was going to be like the fiasco in the computer room.

"I see," he said. He stood up and looked

down at me. "Well, I was just trying to look out for your best interests, Maggie. I just want you to enjoy yourself instead of being miserable. Don't say I didn't warn you."

I sighed happily. He was only looking out for my interests. He wanted me to enjoy myself and be happy. What a good sign! What a great guy!

"You want to borrow *how* much?" Les asked, sounding surprised. We were standing in front of the Banana Republic display window, in the mall. It was Saturday morning, just one week before the first orienteering practice meet.

"Only twenty-five dollars," I said. "That's all." I looked at the display. "And if you ask me, it's a real bargain."

"What is it?" Les asked, staring at it. "And why has it got all those pockets?"

"Why, it's a safari jacket, of course. Isn't it neat? And the pockets are where you're supposed to put the things you need when you go out on safari—compass, flashlight, binoculars, map, canteen, food, first-aid kit, mosquito netting. Why, with a jacket like this, I wouldn't need a backpack. And it looks great, too, don't you think? Sort of like *Out of Africa*."

I sighed, imagining myself as Meryl

Streep and Adam as Robert Redford, trekking off into the jungle on a romantic safari with our faithful bearers following behind, carrying our guns and tents and dinner, with a bottle of vintage champagne. No, make that two bottles of vintage champagne. And at dawn I would shoot a lion and Adam would present the pelt to me. . . .

"Now, wait a minute, Maggie," Les objected. "You're not going to Africa. You're only going on a one-day practice meet at the Black Swamp Boy Scout Camp."

"Well, maybe so. But it won't hurt to be prepared. Besides, I really like the way the jacket looks. I think Adam will be impressed."

"Yes, but twenty-five dollars . . ."

I looked at Les sidelong. "Don't you owe me something for all those times I've helped you baby-sit with the Royal Pain?"

Les looked thoughtful. "I guess you're right," she said finally. She dug into her purse to find her wallet. "But it's just a loan, remember. I'm not giving it to you."

"That's fine. I'll pay you back," I promised. It was a phrase I was getting used to.

When I got home with my jacket and tried it on again, it still looked great. There were pockets on the front, pockets on the sleeves, and pockets on the inside—and even on the back!

Frog and Doodle came in when I was standing in front of the mirror.

"Hey, that's a neat jacket," Frog said. He sat down cross-legged on the floor, and Doodle crawled into his lap and fell asleep almost immediately. "What's it for?"

"It's a safari jacket," I told him. "It's what you wear when you go on safari to Africa."

Frog looked interested. "You're going to Africa? How come you didn't tell us about it at dinner last night? Wow, a safari. That sounds really cool."

"Well, I'm not going on a safari, and I'm not going to Africa. But the Orienteering Club at school is going to the Black Swamp Boy Scout Camp for a practice meet—and I'm in it."

"Oh, yeah?" Frog said, even more interested. "That's where all the *snakes* are."

I shuddered. I had told Adam the truth. I wasn't afraid of snakes. But I didn't exactly go out of my way to find them, either. I still remembered all the snake identifications I'd had to do for my Ecology badge—that was enough to last me a lifetime.

Frog pointed to a loop on my jacket. "What are you supposed to put in that?"

"That's for a hatchet, I think," I said.

"And that one?"

"That's where you put your flashlight." I showed him another pocket. "And here's where you put your compass, and this is where you keep your first-aid kit and—"

"Do you have a compass?" Frog interrupted.

I stared at him, my mouth hanging open. I'd forgotten the most important thing. What else didn't I have?

Frog told me. "How about a flashlight? And a first-aid kit?"

I felt so stupid. Here I'd been, so excited about my new jacket with all its wonderful pockets, that I hadn't stopped to think whether I had anything to put in them. At the very least, I had to have a compass. I couldn't go orienteering without a compass.

I made a list in my head of what I would need, and how much everything would cost. If I bought just the bare essentials, it would be about ten or fifteen dollars total. I didn't even know if I had fifteen cents. I looked at Frog as lovingly as I could look at an obnoxious eleven-year-old brother.

"Frog, what would you think if—"

Frog scrambled to his feet and Doodle fell out of his lap with a thud. "Not on your life," Frog said flatly. Doodle gave a mournful little bark and left the room, looking offended. "I'm not loaning you any more money. You still owe me from the last time, remember? And the interest is piling up."

"How could I forget?" I sighed. Anyway, it wasn't a good idea to borrow any more money. As it was, I was in hock up to my eyebrows. It would be next Christmas—no, probably Christmas *after* next—by the time I paid off Frog and Les and started getting allowance money of my own again.

Dejected, I stared at myself in the mirror. Here I was, with my spiffy new safari jacket, and nothing to put in the pockets. "What am I going to do?" I muttered. "I mean, I *have* to have a compass, at least."

"Maybe you don't have to buy one; maybe you could borrow one," Frog suggested. "Do you know anybody who's got a compass they could loan you?"

I looked at Frog. "As a matter of fact, I do," I said.

Chapter Ten

Sam's house was only about three blocks from mine, so it just took a minute to hop on my bike and ride over there. I didn't give myself time to think about how I was going to feel, seeing Sam after what had happened in the computer room. As far as I was concerned, that was something I wanted to forget. I hoped that Sam had already forgotten it, too.

Nobody at the Tildens' answered my knock on the front door, so I went around the house and into the backyard. Sam was just climbing out of the pool. He was wearing a pair of white swimming trunks. I was surprised to notice how brown he was—and how muscular. The last time I'd bothered to look at Sam's muscles, a couple of years before at the pool, there hadn't been any to look at. Since then, I'd only seen him with his shirt on.

"I—I didn't mean to interrupt your swimming," I said, staring at him. I'd never stared at Sam Tilden before, but then, seeing him in his swimming trunks was a little unexpected.

"Oh, that's okay," Sam said, rubbing his brown hair with a towel. He gestured toward a chair. "Sit down, won't you? I was just finishing up. I do laps every day. I'm up to seventy-five now."

I nodded, impressed. Seventy-five laps! So that's where the muscles came from. Obviously, he wasn't living in his math book anymore. And from the looks of his tan, he'd have to be spending as much time in the sun as he was spending in the pool.

"Uh, well, I can't stay," I said. "I just dropped over to ask you something."

"Okay, ask," Sam said. He draped the towel over his shoulders and put on a pair of sunglasses—the shiny metallic wrap-around kind. I was surprised at how different they made him look—how much older, especially now that his braces had disappeared. "Say, would you like some iced tea or a soda or something?"

"Iced tea would be nice," I said. "I've been riding my bike and it's kind of warm."

"Sure. Come on."

We went into the kitchen and Sam got us two iced teas and then we went back out and sat at a table beside the pool, under the shade of a big umbrella.

"So what did you want to ask?" Sam prompted.

For some reason I felt a little shy. I guess it was because Sam looked so different, in his swimming trunks and those sunglasses, with the towel draped around his neck like one of the hunks at the beach. He didn't look like himself—he looked too cute. I wondered why I hadn't noticed before just how cute he was, although Les apparently had. Then I began to feel disloyal to Adam, and I pushed any thoughts of Sam out of my mind. But I still felt a little funny, as if the Sam Tilden I was talking to wasn't the same boy I'd grown up with. That was probably how he'd felt about me when I wore black and dyed my hair pink. What was happening to us? I'd heard high school was weird, but not *this* weird.

I finally managed to say something after taking a huge sip of iced tea. "Well, uh, I was wondering if you'd mind . . . That is, I need to borrow a compass, and I was remembering that you—"

"Oh, you want my old Boy Scout compass," Sam said, pushing his glasses up on top of his head. He had been a member of the Boy Scouts a couple of years ago. He used to wear his uniform to school sometimes. Sam glanced at me curiously. "What do you need a compass for?"

I cleared my throat. "I . . . well, I've just joined the Orienteering Club, and . . ." My voice trailed off.

Sam looked at me. He raised one eyebrow. "Isn't that the club that Adam DeLong is organizing?" he asked.

I tried to look surprised. "He is?" I mumbled. "I mean, I guess I heard that someplace or another, but—" It hadn't occurred to me how awkward it would be to ask Sam to loan me his compass so I could impress Adam, but all of a sudden it felt awkward. I picked up my iced tea to take a drink and cover my confusion. But my hand slipped on the wet glass and I dropped it with a crash. The iced tea cascaded right into Sam's lap.

"Oh, gosh, I'm sorry, Sam, I don't know what happened, I—" I jumped up and began to look for something to mop up the mess. "I'm just the biggest klutz lately! I'm really sorry," I said.

"Oh, that's okay," he said in a cheerful voice. "I'm already wet, remember?" He pulled the towel off his neck and dried himself and then wiped off the table.

When he'd finished, he turned back to me. "A compass, huh? So you're planning to show Adam how well you can follow a map?"

My cheeks were burning. "Well, not exactly," I lied. "I mean, I . . . . " I gave up explaining why I was doing orienteering. He knew the reason why. "Could I borrow it?" I asked. "The compass, I mean."

Sam had that twinkle in his eyes that he seemed to have a lot, lately. "Sure. Come on," he said as he stood up.

Still blushing, I followed him into the garage, where he pulled down a big box of stuff—in it were his Scout uniform and a bunch of other outdoorsy-type things.

"Here's the compass," he said, rummaging in the box. "Do you know how to use it?"

I nodded. "I learned how when I got my Finding Your Way badge in the Girl Scouts."

Sam handed me a marking pen. "Let me show you an old Boy Scout trick," he said. "When you're out on a course, you jot down the compass headings on the back of your hand as you go along. That way, even if you lose your map, you won't lose your way."

I took the pen. "Good idea," I said,

impressed. I hadn't realized that Sam was so resourceful.

"Where's Adam taking you off to?" Sam asked, going back to the box.

"The first club meet," I said stiffly, "is at the Black Swamp Camp."

The corner of Sam's mouth twitched. "Then it wouldn't hurt to take my old snakebite kit," he said. He tossed me what looked like two little rubber thimbles stuck together.

I looked at it. "You mean, there really *are* snakes out there—poisonous ones? Not that I'm afraid of them, I mean," I added hastily. "I'm just curious."

"Sure there are snakes out there. Mostly they stay away from you—they're more afraid of you than you are of them. But as a former Girl Scout, I'm sure you know the motto—Be Prepared."

"Yeah. Thanks," I said. He ws right, it was better to be safe than sorry. Besides, I had all those pockets—I might as well fill them up, or I'd look stupid.

Sam pulled something else out of the box. "And here's a first-aid kit— it's got a magnifying glass and some tweezers in it, in case you have to pull out a splinter or something. And my old canteen, and a whistle, and some extra-powerful mosquito repellant, specially formulated for Black Swamp mosquitoes. Do you think you could use any of this?"

I accepted everything Sam offered me gladly. I was definitely going to look like a serious orienteerer, if there was such a word, with all these wonderful gadgets sticking out of the pockets of my safari jacket. I wasn't sure what I'd need a whistle for, but it was on this neat-looking strip of leather. It would look perfect around my neck.

"Gosh, Sam, I don't know how to thank you," I said, holding all the stuff in my hands. The line sounded familiar, and I realized I had said the same thing to Sam after he fixed the can of hair spray, just before I gave him that silly, impulsive kiss. But he'd been terrific to loan me all these things. He didn't have to. He'd been awfully nice about my spilling tea on him, too. And he hadn't mentioned the scene in the computer room even once.

Sam looked at me. "Another kiss, maybe?" he asked lightly. "I kind of liked the first one."

So Sam hadn't forgotten. The color began to rise up in my cheeks. I didn't know what to say. Kissing him in the hallway was one thing. Kissing him in the garage, in private, especially with his shirt off and those gorgeous muscles showing, was quite another.

Sam cleared his throat. "That's okay, Mag," he said. "You don't have to." He looked intently at me. "Look, in my opinion, just in case it means anything to you, Adam DeLong has very large rocks in his oversize head if he doesn't like you already. I wouldn't worry about proving yourself on this trip. I don't even know why you're going, but I hope you have fun," he said, not very convincingly.

I gulped. "Gee, thanks," I mumbled. If it were anybody else but Sam Tilden, I might have said he sounded jealous.

At school that week, there was an organizational meeting for the Orienteering Club in the gym. About thirty of us were there. I was glad to see that there were only a half dozen girls in the group—and that Jennifer wasn't one of them. That meant that there was an even greater chance that I could get Adam's attention.

Mr. Cowper started things off by giving us a list of the things we needed to bring, like a compass and a canteen and a whistle. Then he turned the meeting over to Adam, who announced that we should all be at school at seven A.M. sharp on Saturday morning to catch the bus to the Black Swamp Camp.

"Seven A.M.!" one of the boys moaned. "What is this, the army?"

Adam looked at him sternly. "The bus is leaving promptly at five after seven," he said. "Anybody who gets there late gets *left*." He started to pass out sheets of paper. "This is a release," he said. "You're supposed to take it home and ask your parents to sign it."

I looked at the paper. It looked like a legal document. "What does it say?" I asked.

Adam glanced at me. "It says that if you hurt yourself out on the trail," he said very distinctly, "the school isn't responsible."

"Say, Adam," another boy asked, "what is this? The Bataan Death March? I mean, I thought we were in this to have fun."

Adam looked at the boy and frowned. "Listen, Charlie," he said, "this is serious stuff. If you don't know what you're doing, the wilderness can be a dangerous place. Believe me, I speak from experience." He glanced around the room. "I have a feeling," he added, dropping his voice a notch, "that some of you think this is just a game. You're in it for the laughs. But I want you to know that it's the real thing. Out there in the woods, you never know what's going to happen. It's every man for himself. It's raw survival, that's what it is."

I felt a thrill go through my veins. Adam's little speech had been so incredibly exhilarating; he made it sound so exciting. I felt like I wanted to charge right out into the jungle and pit myself against the forces of nature.

There was a murmur in the group. "Go get 'em, Rambo," somebody muttered.

Mr. Cowper stood up and held up his hand. "Of course," he said soothingly, "we don't expect any serious problems. After all, the courses we'll be using for our meet have been set up by qualified and experienced professionals. As long as you stay on the course, you shouldn't run into any problems. But accidents do happen occasionally, and that's why we need your parents to sign the release."

I put the release in my purse. Well, if an accident did happen, I, for one, would be prepared. I had Sam's first-aid kit tucked into one of the pockets of my safari jacket.

Chapter Eleven

"But I don't *want* to go to the swimming meet!" I said. "How come I have to do it?" I put down my fork and looked at Frog. "And how come he gets to wear his swim goggles at the table?"

Mom looked mildly amazed. "Because I didn't notice that he had them on," she said. "Frog, take off your goggles. You know you're not supposed to wear them at the dinner table." She turned to me. "And you get to go to Frog's swimming meet tomorrow night, Maggie, because everybody else in the family is busy." She began ticking things off on her fingers. "I've got an extra taping for the show. Your father has a symphony performance, and the other cellist is sick, so he can't get out of it. And Ellyn has—" She looked at Ellyn. "I forget. What are you doing, Ellyn?"

Ellyn looked up from her meat loaf. "It's the organizational meeting for the yearbook," she said, in an important voice. "I can't possibly miss it. I'm in charge of running it!"

"And it's a big night for Frog," my father pointed out cheerily. "Somebody from the family has to be there to cheer him on when he's getting to the finish line." He patted Frog's shoulder. "We want Frog to do the very best job he can possibly do, don't we? How can he do that if his family isn't behind him a hundred percent?"

"But Les and I were planning to go to the movies tomorrow night," I objected. The Royal Pain was out of town with his parents, and Les had won two free tickets in a giveaway at the grocery store. Getting a free ticket was the only way I could go anywhere these days. I was thinking of bringing my old clothes to a thrift shop and seeing how much I could get for them.

My father grinned. "The movies will be there next week," he said. "Take Les with you. It'll be a lot of fun. You'll see some terrific swimming. After all, it is the district meet."

I groaned. I was sure that the last thing Les would want to do on Friday evening was to hang out with a bunch of soggy eleven-year-olds. It was certainly the last thing I wanted to do.

"Good," my mother said, beaming happily. "So it's all settled. Maggie and Les will be Frog's cheering section. Now, how about seconds on cauliflower?"

After supper, I called Les. "You won't believe this," I said woefully, "but our movie date's been canceled. I have to go to Frog's swimming meet."

"Oh, no," Les said. "The tickets are only good for tomorrow night."

I sighed. "Then I guess you'll have to get somebody else to go with you."

"Wait a minute," Les said. "Are you talking about the district swimming meet? That's tomorrow night?"

"I guess so," I said. "Yeah, I guess that's what it is." What did it matter? A swimming meet was a swimming meet, wasn't it? It was nothing but a bunch of little kids wearing goggles thrashing around in the swimming pool, while parents and other unfortunate family members like me sat cheering on the sidelines.

Les was silent for a minute. "Well, then, maybe I will go," she said. "I can probably trade the tickets to Mary Louise for one of her new novels."

I was practically in shock. I had already resigned myself to the idea of going by myself. "You *will*?" I said gratefully.

"Gosh, that's terrific, Les." At least I wouldn't have to suffer alone.

"What do you think we should wear?"

"Wear?" I gave a short laugh. "What does it matter what we wear to a swimming meet? Are you trying to impress an eleven-year-old or something?"

"I think," she said reflectively, "I'll wear my new gray slacks."

The meet was held at the indoor municipal pool downtown. By the time Les and I got there, the bleachers were already pretty crowded. I bought a bag of popcorn and Les got a candy bar and we sat down on the top row, way at the back.

"I wonder how come there are so many people," I said idly, beginning to munch my popcorn. There was already a group of swimmers lined up on the side, younger kids, and then there was a whistle and an enormous splash, and kids started racing across the pool with a great flurry of arms and legs.

"Because it's district, dummy," Les said. She straightened her new pink-and-gray striped blouse and pointed up to the board. "See? There are competitions in all the age divisions. It's not just the elevens and twelves."

"Oh, yeah," I said. I checked the board. "Well, it looks like Frog's division will be coming up next. After that we can go." I looked down at my watch. "Hey, if we can get the right bus, we can probably make the nine o'clock movie."

"Nope," Les said briefly, still studying the board. "We can't."

"We can't? How come? Did you trade the tickets to Mary Louise?"

"We can't go because I want to watch the older division," Les said, settling back into her seat and unwrapping her candy bar. "The fifteen- and sixteen-year-old class is coming up in an hour or so and I don't want to miss it."

I stared at her. "Why all this sudden interest in swimming?" I asked. Then I thought of something. "Ah-ha!" I exclaimed. "So *that's* why you got dressed up for the occasion. Who is he?"

Les blushed pinker than her blouse. "Nobody," she said.

I stared at her. "You won't tell me?" I asked, "After all we've been through together? Leslie Langsdorf, I thought we were best friends."

"There's nothing to tell," Les said. She put her hand over her heart. "Honest."

"I can see," I said stiffly, "that you just

don't trust me. Even though I've confided in you about every minor detail of *my* crush."

Les turned around to face me. "It's not a matter of trust," she said. "I just don't want to talk about it. I mean, you're still my best friend and all that, but I don't want to talk about it. Okay?" She grabbed my arm and pointed. "Isn't that Frog down there, getting lined up at the edge of the pool? Shouldn't we go sit where he can hear us yell?"

So I gave up trying to get her to tell me who she was dying to see, and we climbed down the bleachers to the front row, right behind the swimmers. Frog was there, jumping up and down, twisting his arms and wiggling his hands the way swimmers do when they're warming up.

"Hey, Frog!" I shouted, when all the kids lined up at the edge of the pool. "Go for it! You can do it!" He turned around and flashed me a thumbs-up signal and a big smile.

I have to admit, I *was* pretty proud when Frog came in first. In fact, by the time he was on his last lap, I was standing up, waving my arms and screaming at the top of my lungs. And when it was all over and Frog had beaten all the other eleven-year-olds, I collapsed onto my seat. I would have vaulted over the rail and hugged him, dripping swimsuit and goggles and all, but the sign on the rail said Spectators Stay Back.

"I guess I'm glad I came," I said to Les, as we went to get something to drink. "Frog is a pretty decent brother, all things considered." I paid for my soda and waited while Les bought one for herself.

"So you're not bummed out any more?" Les asked. "About not winning first place in things or getting elected to be queen of some country?"

"Oh, I still get bummed out when I think about it," I told her. "But after tomorrow . . ." We sat back down and sipped our sodas while I thought about my new safari jacket and all the equipment I'd borrowed from Sam, and how impressive that outfit was going to look on me. "After tomorrow," I assured Les, "everything in my life is going to be different."

Les gave me a look. "Oh, yeah. Tomorrow is the day that you show Adam how great you are in the wilderness." She giggled. "A real female Daniel Boone, huh?"

I nodded. "Yeah. After tomorrow—" I stopped, surprised. "Hey, isn't that Sam?"

I looked again. It *was* Sam, wearing the same white swimming trunks he'd been wearing when I'd seen him at his pool the week before. Seeing him reminded me of what had gone on in his garage, when I'd been tempted to kiss him, and I could feel my cheeks beginning to get pink. I didn't know he was swimming in competition. He hadn't said anything about it. But then, that was Sam. He was a very modest kind of person.

"Sam?" Les said quickly, looking around. "You mean, Sam Tilden?"

I nodded, almost wishing that I hadn't pointed him out. What if she asked him to come over? What would I say to him? Could I stop blushing before he got here, or would it get worse?

"Oh, it is Sam!" Les said happily. "Wow," she breathed. "Just look at those muscles. You know, you'd never guess from just looking at him that he's wearing all those muscles under his shirt. And now that he's got his braces off, he's so cute." Les leaned forward and cupped her hands around her mouth like a megaphone. "Hey, Sam!" she yelled. "Good luck!"

I was so embarrassed. Did she have to let everyone in the entire town know we were there? And now Sam would have to come over. I sank down in my seat, a feeling of dread settling over me like a cloud of pink hair spray.

Sam looked up at Les and me, as if he were surprised to see us. And just at that moment, Frog came up and sat down beside me, his hair still slightly damp from the pool and a big smile splitting his face. Sam stepped closer to the railing and grinned at Frog.

"Hey, kid, that was a pretty impressive time you put in tonight," he said. He reached over the rail and ruffled Frog's hair in a friendly, big-brotherly way. "Good going, Frog."

"Yeah, thanks, Sam," Frog said in the most modest voice I had ever heard him use. "Maybe next year I'll beat *you*, huh?" Then he frowned a little. "Better make that two years, maybe. Let's see, in two years I'll be thirteen and you'll be—" He turned to me, distressed. "I'll probably never catch up with Sam, no matter how old I get!"

Sam laughed. "Maybe not. But you'll be way ahead of all the other thirteen-year-olds—just wait and see. This time next year, your times will be even better."

Frog sat back, looking pleased by the compliment. Sam turned to Les and me.

"I'm glad you guys decided to hang around," he said quietly. "It's nice to have a cheering section."

I shifted uncomfortably, feeling the blush rise higher in my cheeks. Did he think I'd stayed around just to see him swim? But I didn't have to answer because Les spoke right up. I relaxed and sipped on my drink, until I heard what she was saying.

"Yeah, we were going to leave. But when Maggie found out that you were swimming tonight, she insisted that we wait around and watch," she said.

I choked on a piece of ice, and Frog pounded me a couple of times on the back. I tried to smile as if nothing had happened. I could feel the ice cube melting in my throat.

"You did, huh?" Sam looked at me with that familiar twinkle in his eyes. "Thanks a lot. I wish I could ask you girls out for a soda or something after the meet, but my mom's picking me up and I promised I'd be—"

"Oh, that's all right," I said hastily, putting down my drink. "In fact, we weren't waiting for any particular division." I stood up and looked down at Les, giving her one of those I-can't-believe-you-just-did-that looks. "We can go any time you're ready, Les," I said.

Les grinned. "Let's wait until after this race, okay? Good luck, Sam!" she called, as the coach signaled for Sam to line up. "We're rooting for you!"

Best friend? I could have killed her. What guy was so important to her that she had to embarrass me in front of Sam? Was she trying to get the guy's attention by talking to Sam, make him jealous or something? Or was *Sam* the guy she wanted to see? I wasn't sure, as I watched her watch Sam dive into the water. She sure wasn't interested in telling me, anyway.

I had set the alarm clock for six on Saturday morning, just to make sure I had plenty of time to get ready for the big meet. Of course, nobody else was up at that hour, except for my mother, who was leaving for the studio. So I ate a bowl of cereal all by myself and thought about Sam and how cute he'd looked. I was worried that he might think I'd gone to the meet just to see him. I mean, it had been really neat to watch him win and see everybody congratulate him, but I wouldn't want him to think that I was hanging around just for him. Anyway, I had more pressing things to worry about than Sam Tilden—Adam, and getting to school by seven o'clock, for instance. So, with Doodle's supervision, I fixed a couple of jelly-and-cream-cheese sandwiches for lunch, which I packed along with an apple and a few of Mom's ginger cookies. Then I filled my canteen and put a couple of ice cubes in it.

After that, Doodle and I went back upstairs and I put my safari jacket on over my T-shirt and jeans and began loading up the pockets. After a long and serious discussion with myself, I'd decided to wear jeans instead of shorts. I hate it when the mosquitoes bite my knees, and even though I had plenty of Sam's repellant, it was better to be on the safe side.

"What are you doing?" Ellyn asked from the other bed, rolling over sleepily. She opened one bleary eye to look at the clock. "Good Lord, Margaret. It's only six fifteen."

"I have to catch the bus at seven," I told her. "We're going up to Black Swamp Camp for an orienteering meet."

"That snaky place?" Ellyn shuddered. "You wouldn't catch me going up there."

I was beginning to wish that everybody wouldn't talk about all the snakes, but I only shrugged. "I've got a snakebite kit," I said, putting it into my pocket. "Just in case. And I'm wearing my boots." Not my pink boots, but my old hiking boots. The ones I got two years ago, when Dad took us hiking in the Smokies. I wasn't taking any chances.

Ellyn turned over. "Well, watch out for the crocodiles," she said.

"Alligators," I corrected her crossly. "Crocodiles live in Africa." Why couldn't people get that one simple little fact straight?

"Well, whatever." Ellyn's voice was muffled by her pillow. "Watch out for them anyway. You wouldn't want one to eat your foot, would you?"

"No," I said, frowning at Doodle, who was settling down for a nap on my pink sweatshirt. "I've already lost one boot to an animal in the last two weeks."

Mornings in our part of Florida are sometimes kind of cool and breezy, but this particular morning was hot and muggy, even at seven A.M. and the sun was already fierce. The thirty or so kids gathered in the parking lot were wearing shorts and T-shirts and some of them had on sandals. Almost all of them had backpacks. I felt a little conspicuous in my safari jacket and jeans and my hiking boots.

"How come you're wearing that long-sleeved jacket?" Brenda Bixby asked while we were standing around waiting for the bus.

Brenda Bixby isn't one of my favorite people. She's only thirteen, but she's already in high school because she got put ahead a year for being smart. The kids call her Brenda the Brat, and she doesn't have a lot of friends. I guess that's why she joins so many clubs.

"Because," I said loftily, keeping my eye out for Adam. "Because I want to."

"That's not a good enough reason," Brenda objected. "The meteorologist on the Morning Report said it's going to be in the nineties today, and the humidity is already over eighty percent. You're going to sweat to death. Maybe you'd better leave it on the bus."

It felt like it was ninety already, and the humidity inside my safari jacket made it seem more like a hundred and twenty. But I couldn't leave it on the bus. Where would I carry my compass and my first-aid kit—not to mention my lunch? Anyway, this was the day I'd been waiting for; the day I was going to make up for the horrible impression I'd left on Adam the week before. I wasn't going to let a little thing like a heat stroke bother me.

I ignored Brenda and kept on looking for Adam. You see, I had this plan. I was going to stand right behind Adam when the bus came, and then follow him onto the bus so I could sit beside him. It was nearly an hour's drive to Black Swamp Camp. A whole hour sitting beside Adam DeLong! It would be ecstasy. It would be a great beginning for what I just knew was going to be a wonderful day—the start of a whole new relationship between Adam and me. I pushed the thought of Sam Tilden out of my mind. Why should I worry about what he thought? Les was the one who'd wanted to hang around, not me. Maybe I should tell him that, the next time I saw him.

I looked at my watch for the third time. It was four minutes after seven and the bus, with Mr. Cowper on it, was just pulling up in front of us. Where was Adam? Behind me, a couple of boys were talking.

"Yeah, well, personally, I think it would be pretty hilarious if he missed the bus," one of them was saying.

"Right," the other one agreed. "Especially after he made such a big deal about everybody being on time. If he's not here in sixty seconds, I vote we drive off and leave him."

I was about to turn around and defend Adam when a car drove up. I stepped forward expectantly, my spirits soaring. Yes, it was Adam. And then Jennifer got out of the car, right behind him. The day was not getting off to a good start. Both of them were dressed in white shorts and white T-shirts, wearing white tennis sneakers and white socks. They looked like they belonged in one of those ritzy tennis club advertisements, where everybody's sitting around sipping drinks after an hour on the court.

"Okay, people," Adam said, waving his hands the way a teacher did when he wanted to control a class on field trip. "Line up. Let's get this show on the road."

I lined up, but there wasn't any point in trying to stand behind Adam. Not with Jennifer there. And as for sitting next to him on the bus—*ha ha*. Guess who I got to sit with? Yes, that's right, I got to sit with Brenda the Brat, as I sweltered in my safari jacket. Such ecstasy.

Chapter Twelve

"Okay, everybody, over here."

We were all piling out of the bus at Black Swamp Camp. Around us loomed what looked to me like a very dense jungle of slash pines and live oaks covered with gray Spanish moss, all matted together with vines, some of which, I was sure, was poison ivy.

"You mean, we're going to have to hike through *that* stuff?" Brenda asked, at my elbow. She was staring into the jungle, panic in her eyes.

"You could always stay on the bus," I said.

Brenda stepped closer to me. "How about if you and I go as partners?" she asked. "I mean, we do this in teams, don't we?"

I sighed. The last thing I wanted was to be teamed up with Brenda. But short of telling her bluntly that I didn't want to be her partner, I couldn't see any way out of it.

"I guess so," I said glumly. Anyway, with Jennifer along, my chances for getting any time alone with Adam had vanished totally. I had wasted Les's twenty-five dollars on a safari jacket that was too hot, only to be sent into the jungle with the world's worst complainer.

Mr. Cowper waved at Brenda and me. "If you girls are going out on the course, you'd better get over here and get your instructions first."

Adam was standing on a picnic table so that everyone could see him. It wasn't really necessary since we could all see him just fine, but I guess he wanted everyone to know that he was the leader of the pack. Anyway, it was okay with me if Adam wanted to stand on the table. I was amazed by the fact that I was looking right at his knees. I'd never seen them at eye-level before. They looked strange, but then, so do everyone's. And he had the cutest little scar. I wondered if it was from a previous orienteering outing. He'd probably fought with some sort of wild animal.

"In a few minutes," he began, sounding like a drill instructor, "I'm going to give everybody their course and starting time assignments. But first let's review the way this meet is supposed to work." He paused to slap at a mosquito on his thigh. "There are three courses, of three miles each," he went on. "They've already been laid out by the people here at the Boy Scout camp, and they're marked with colored markers every quarter of a mile along the way. That means that each course will consist of twelve markers, including the finish. There are no paths, but we've been assured that the markers are clearly visible—as long as you stay on the course, that is."

"No paths!" somebody exclaimed, in a horrified tone. "What do we walk on?"

"We walk on our *feet*, you idiot," somebody else answered scornfully. "Through the wilderness. Like in *The Last of the Mohicans*."

Adam ignored the interruption. "We'll work in teams of two," he continued. "Each team is assigned a course and a starting time, at half-hour intervals. I'll give you a map that's got the course and compass directions drawn on it. Your team uses your compass and your map-reading skills to get from one marker to another, around the course. The object is to get back to the start in the shortest possible time."

Next to me, Brenda raised her hand.

"But what if we get lost?" she asked timidly. It was the first time I'd ever heard Brenda sound timid about anything.

Adam shrugged. "The object is not to get lost," he said, with an unsympathetic frown in Brenda's direction. "Anybody who gets lost probably doesn't belong in the Orienteering Club."

Mr. Cowper stepped forward. "That's what your whistle is for," he told us. "If you can't find the next marker and you think you're lost, stay put. Don't move around and don't panic. Blow two blasts on your whistle every minute until somebody finds you. But don't use the whistle unless it's an emergency. Okay?"

I fingered Sam's whistle, hanging around my neck like a charm. It reminded me of Sam. I hoped I wouldn't need it, but it felt reassuring to have it anyway. Maybe it would bring me good luck.

Mr. Cowper took out a piece of paper. "I have the team assignments now, if you're all ready." A general grumble went around the group.

"Team assignments?" one of the boys asked. "You mean, we don't get to choose our own partners?"

Mr. Cowper shook his head. "It's fairer if you're randomly matched," he said. "That keeps you hot-shot hikers from pairing up on an easy trail and wiping out everybody else." There was laughter from the group. Mr. Cowper looked around. "In order to make sure that there's no bias in these assignments, Adam has created a computer program that has random-matched all your names and assigned you to a trail. I ran the program last night, and not even Adam has seen the results."

My face, which was already red from the heat, got even redder. The program he was talking about must have been the file that I had wiped out the other day. But apparently Adam had gotten the program working again, because Mr. Cowper was reading out the names of the teams.

"Brenda Bixby and Michael Kennedy will take the Palmetto Ridge Trail," he said.

Beside me, Brenda grinned happily. "Wow," she whispered, "that means I get to go with a *boy*!"

"Great," I whispered back. It was good news—at least I wouldn't be stuck with her. Somewhere in the back of the crowd Michael Kennedy moaned loudly.

"Jennifer Blair and Rod Haynes will take the White-tail Deer Trail," Mr. Cowper announced.

Jennifer smiled and Rod Haynes held up his hands in a gesture of victory. "You and me'll wipe 'em out, hot-shot," he told Jennifer. Everybody laughed. I laughed, too. If I didn't get to go with Adam, at least Jennifer didn't either.

Mr. Cowper went on. "Maggie Mason and Adam DeLong will take the Mosquito Bay Trail."

My heart stopped. I mean, it literally stopped, for at least five seconds. I stared at Adam, open-mouthed. Up on the picnic bench, Adam was staring at me. His mouth was open, too. I couldn't believe it. My fondest dream—the dream of spending time with Adam, just the two of us, alone—was about to come true, on the trail to Mosquito Bay! Les's twenty-five dollars hadn't been spent in vain, after all.

Adam and I had been assigned the last start on our particular course, which meant that we didn't get going until after lunch. Just before our starting time, he pulled me aside. I looked at him with great anticipation. My wonderful adventure was about to begin. Surely, along the trail somewhere I would find an opportunity to say, "Excuse me, I love you," as I'd wanted to that day in homeroom.

"All right, Maggie," he said, "here's what

we're going to do." He pulled out a fancy compass and snapped it open. "Since *I* know how to read the compass, I'll take the compass readings and sight landmarks along our course." He showed me a thing that looked like a watch, hanging from his belt. "I'm wearing a pedometer, so we'll know how far we've come and when to start looking for the next mark."

"Super," I said. "What do you want me to do?"

Adam looked at me. "There is something you can do," he said thoughtfully.

"Yes?" I prompted.

"You can try not to get in the way. I mean, this is serious business. We don't need somebody clowning around and getting us into trouble out there."

I sighed. He didn't have to rub it in that I was a klutz, did he? I wanted to tell him that I knew how to read a compass and a map, too, but it didn't seem like the right time, so I kept quiet. I'd get to show him what I could do once we were out on the trail.

Adam tried to swat a mosquito that was buzzing around his head. "And remember, this is a race, and we're in it to win. We have to move at a fast pace. I hope you can keep up with me."

"Yes," I said. I had to suppress the urge to say "Yes, *sir*!" Adam was sounding more and more like an army sergeant all the time. But I wouldn't let him down. I'd follow his orders. I would stay out of his way, and I would keep up. And by the time we got back, he would be super-impressed with my courage and my stamina and all the things I knew about the wilderness.

Mr. Cowper waved to us, to let us know that it was our turn to start. "Okay, team," he said, holding up his stopwatch. "Remember that you're starting last, and there won't be anybody behind you on the trail. Try extra-hard not to get lost, huh?"

Adam grinned confidently at Mr. Cowper. "Who, *us*? Hey, we're not going to get lost, we're going to win. Aren't we, partner?"

I nodded. "We sure are," I said, trying to match Adam's confidence.

Mr. Cowper clicked his stopwatch. "Okay. I'll see you guys when you get back. Good luck."

Chapter Thirteen

The first two markers, yellow ribbons tied to a couple of trees at eye level, weren't at all hard to find. When Adam wasn't looking, I took Sam's advice and jotted down the compass headings on the back of my hand. Since Adam was carrying the map, I thought maybe I ought to have a record of where we'd been, just in case Adam ditched me and I had to find my way back all by myself.

But if the rest of the course was like this, I told myself as I followed Adam through the woods, it would be simple. The trees were mostly pine, and they were so close together that the needles smothered out most of the underbrush, which made it easy to walk around. The only things you had to watch out for were the spiky palmettos that had a tendency to scratch your face and arms—and, of course, the mosquitoes. The mosquitoes were really fierce.

"Ouch!" Adam said, for the ninth or

tenth time, killing the ninth or tenth mosquito. I looked at him. His face was pink, and he had huge drops of sweat on his forehead. There was a long red gash down one arm where a limb had scratched him and another on his left leg.

"I hate mosquitoes," he snarled. "We never had to fight mosquitoes when our orienteering club went on meets back in California."

"I wonder," I said, to take his mind off what he was missing in California, "what Mosquito Bay is like."

Adam studied the map. "We'll find out soon enough. It's exactly one mile from here," he replied, after a minute. "On some sort of lake. According to the map, our course follows a stream."

"That's good," I offered helpfully. "That probably means easier walking."

"No, that's bad," Adam said. "Walking by a stream means we'll be bombarded by mosquitoes the whole way." He glared at me. "How come they're not biting you?"

"I guess because I'm wearing jeans and a long-sleeved jacket," I answered. In spite of the heat, I was glad I had worn jeans. At least the mosquitoes weren't feasting on my knees, the way they would be if I'd worn shorts. "And a friend gave me this sure-fire mosquito repellant, specially formulated for Black Swamp mosquitoes. It seems to work."

Adam looked harassed as he swatted another one. "I put on some repellant before I left home. But it must have worn off. Besides, it wasn't the deep-forest kind. I didn't expect so many mosquitoes."

I stared at him. Not expect mosquitoes? Where did he think he was, Arizona? "Well, I have some extra if you want some," I offered, taking Sam's repellant out of one of my pockets. Without a word, Adam took it and began to smear it on his bare legs, and we set off again.

The third and fourth markers were a little harder to find. The pines had disappeared and there were lots of alder bushes growing up in dense, tangled thickets, which meant that Adam's pedometer wasn't much good, because we had to go around the thickets and it was harder to tell how far we'd really come. There were palmettos and prickly vines, too, that snatched at you when you tried to push through them. I was glad that I was wearing my safari jacket, which was made of something that the prickles couldn't poke through.

"Ow!" Adam said. He was trying to brush past a springy vine, but it was stuck to his arm. "Hey, that hurts!"

I looked at his arm where the vine had pricked him. The sleeve of his white T-shirt was torn, and the shirt itself was soaked with sweat. "I think maybe you've got a thorn in your arm," I said sympathetically.

"Oh, great," Adam said, with a weary sigh. "Just great. We never had anything like this back in California." He dropped down onto a log and tried to dig the thorn out with his thumbnail. "It's no use," he said. "It's not going to come out."

I reached into another pocket. "Let me try this," I said, pulling out Sam's first-aid kit.

"What've you got there?" Adam asked, suspicious.

"Just a magnifying glass and some tweezers," I said, kneeling down beside him. "Hold still."

I took a deep breath and touched his arm. This time there wasn't any electricity, or tingle. And my hands weren't shaking, either. At least that made it easier to get the thorn out.

"There," I said in my best nurse's voice, when I had pulled out the thorn. "All set. It was just a small thorn."

"It didn't *feel* very small," Adam said. There was a hint of self-pity in his voice. "Do you happen to have any iodine with you?"

"Yes," I said. "Right here." As I was dabbing it on his tiny cut, I had to fight the urge to giggle. After all, it was just a thorn, not a broken arm. Boys were such babies sometimes. But now Adam and I were sort of even, I reasoned. Maybe Adam would forgive me for what had happened in the computer room. Maybe he would even be grateful to me for helping him out.

He stood up and flexed his arm. "Listen, Maggie, we've got to stop wasting time like this," he said, frowning at me. "Remember, this is a race. With all this fooling around, we're going to get beaten for sure."

I sighed and put away Sam's first-aid kit. I wasn't the one who'd made such a big deal about a little pain, I wanted to point out.

When we finally got to the fifth marker, Adam studied the map for a long time. He took out his compass and fiddled with it. I could hear him making some sort of calculation; he was muttering a bunch of numbers.

"What are you doing?" I asked curiously. I looked at the map and noted the bearings of the next couple of markers on the back of my hand.

"I'm figuring out a shortcut," Adam said.

"Hey," I said, "I thought we were supposed to stick to the course."

Adam gave me a look and then shrugged. "The only rule is that we're supposed to get all the way around the course. How we do it is up to us. Of course, we don't have to announce to the entire club that we found a shorter—"

"Are you *sure* it's not cheating?" I asked.

Adam gave this irritating little chuckle, as if I were the most naive person in the world. I wasn't sure I liked that chuckle. "All's fair in love and war," he replied.

"Yeah," I said softly. Where had I heard that before?

He pointed to the map. "What we're going to do," he said, "is to cut off this dogleg. Instead of going from marker five to marker six, we're going from five to seven. It will save us at least fifteen minutes, maybe more."

I frowned at the map. There were some funny little squiggles where Adam was pointing. "Doesn't that route take us right through a swamp?" I asked. "That's what those squiggles mean—swampy territory." I remembered that from when we'd learned to read maps in the Girl Scouts.

Adam folded up the map and stuck it in his back pocket. "Afraid you can't hack it?" he asked. There was that irritating laugh again. Why hadn't I noticed it before? Probably because I'd never talked to him for more than thirty seconds before.

"No," I said slowly, "I'm sure I can hack it. But don't you think we'd better stay on the course? I mean, just to be on the safe side—"

"You can stay on the course if you want," Adam told me. "I'm going to take the shortcut."

"But we're a team," I objected.

"Then all you have to do is stick with me," Adam said confidently. "I know exactly what I'm doing."

I hoped he did. If he didn't, we were going to be in deep trouble.

Half an hour later, I had the feeling that that was exactly where we were. Adam kept checking his compass and muttering something like, "That shouldn't be here," and it was getting awfully swampy. When you put your foot down, there was a sucking sound as you pulled it back up again. I looked at Adam's white tennis sneakers. They weren't white anymore. They were soaking wet and covered with gooey mud. At least my hiking boots, which were a little too hot, were waterproof.

"How far do you think it is to the next marker?" I asked.

Adam shook his head. "The pedometer isn't accurate in this kind of terrain," he said over his shoulder. "But it can't be too far ahead." He tried to grin reassuringly, but his mouth sort of stopped halfway.

The stream we'd been following had broadened into a swamp, littered with enormous fallen cypress logs. We were crossing a narrow inlet of murky brown water on one of these logs, with Adam just in front of me. Somewhere close by I heard a dull, deep, booming sound.

"What's that?" Adam turned around on the log and gestured for me to stand still. He put his hand on my arm and lowered his voice. "Did you hear that noise?"

I nodded, teetering on the log. It was the noise you hear whenever you go walking in the swampy parts of Florida.

I shook off his hand. It wasn't that I didn't want Adam to hold on to me, it was just that I was afraid of losing my balance.

"It's okay," I said, concentrating on not falling off. "You hear it all the time in the swamp."

"But what is it?" he asked, sounding spooked.

I was about to tell him what it was when he grabbed my arm again.

"Look!" he squawked, pointing off toward a cypress stump that stuck out of the brown water about thirty feet away. "Over there! It's a *crocodile*!"

"An alligator," I corrected him automatically. "Crocodiles live in Africa. That's what's making that noise you heard. It's the alligator love song."

At that moment, the alligator opened its mouth in a stupendous yawn, showing its sharp teeth—all of its sharp teeth.

"An alligator!" Adam screeched. He began to teeter on the log.

"It'll go away," I said, trying to calm him down. "They're not aggressive, and they won't attack you unless you bother them."

But Adam wasn't listening. "An alligator!" he screeched again. "Come on, let's get out of here!"

I put out my hand. "Hey, wait, Adam," I said. "Don't be so—"

But just at that moment, Adam lost his balance. His arms began to flail like windmills, he lurched from side to side, and then he fell with a huge splash into the murky brown water of the swamp.

"Help!" he shouted.

I knelt down on the log. "It's okay, Adam," I said, "there goes the alligator. He's swimming away. And it's not very deep here."

But Adam wasn't listening.

"Help!" he shouted frantically, thrashing around in the water like a giant turtle. "Help, Maggie! I can't swim!"

I held out my hand. "It's okay," I repeated. "Really, it's not that deep. All you have to do is stand up." How could he live in California and not know how to swim? I wondered.

"Help!" he cried again. "I'm drowning."

"Adam," I shouted, "for pete's sake, *stand up*!"

He stood up. The water was only up to his waist.

Chapter Fourteen

"So what happened *then*?" my mother asked. She was laughing so hard that the tears were streaming down her cheeks. The two of us were in the kitchen, getting ready for Saturday night's dinner, which at our house is almost always pizza.

"So then Adam whacked the snake," I said with a giggle. "But he didn't kill it. It rolled over and hid in the bushes until we were out of sight. It came back to life after we started to walk away."

"Then what happened?"

"Then when we got back, he told Jennifer it was a *deadly* snake, and that I had been so scared I had almost fainted. And *she* said—"

Mom began to howl again, holding her sides.

"—and *she* said wasn't I lucky to have Adam to protect me." I was laughing, too, so hard that the corners of my mouth hurt, remembering the adoring way Jennifer had looked at Adam. It sort of reminded me of the way I had looked at Adam, up until today. It was good to be able to laugh about it now, especially with my mother.

Mom wiped her eyes. "I guess what I don't understand," she said, "is why you didn't tell on Adam when you heard what he was saying to Jennifer. It would have served him right, wouldn't it?" She gave me a questioning look.

"It's a little hard to explain," I said. "Anyway, it didn't hurt anything to let him tell Jennifer all that stuff. She already thinks he's Superman."

Mom nodded. "So I take it you're no longer carrying a torch for Adam?"

I grinned a little. "Definitely not. I am not even thinking of carrying a torch for Adam."

"So now what?"

"What do you mean, 'now what?'"

"Do you still feel invisible?"

I thought about it. "I guess not," I said. It was a funny thing, but the business with Sam's compass and being able to find my way out of the woods backwards had given me a different feeling about myself. A much better feeling. There probably weren't too many girls in the world who could find their way out of Black Swamp—

or at least there were only a few others in my high school who could do it.

Dad came into the kitchen. "What's all this giggling about?" he asked, pretending to be angry. "Where's my pizza?"

"Howard," my mother told him, "Maggie has the most remarkable story to tell us at dinner."

After dinner was over, I called Les. Her mother answered the phone instead. She sounded a little distracted.

"Les isn't here," she said. "She went over to Sam Tilden's house in the middle of the afternoon, and she's not back yet. I've been calling over there, but the phone's been busy. Listen, Maggie, if you're going over in that direction, would you mind telling her to hurry back home right away?" In the background, I could hear a familiar howling. "Charles is here, and it's time for her father and me to go square dancing." Her voice had a desperate tone to it. "I really need her."

I put down the phone and stared at it. Les had gone over to Sam's house this afternoon? But it was after eight o'clock by now. What were they doing together all this time?

But of course, I already knew the answer to that question, even if I hadn't thought it all out. Les had a crush on Sam! The evidence was all there, if only I'd been looking for it from the time she'd pointed out how cute Sam was without his braces, to the other day at the swimming meet, when she'd wanted to hang around to see his division race. There was a sad, sinking feeling in the pit of my stomach. My very best friend, in love with Sam Tilden—and just at the moment when I'd realized that *I* liked him, too.

Yes, it was true. All my feelings about Adam had just been puppy-love feelings. I realized I had felt about him the same way you feel about handsome movie stars and gorgeous lifeguards you see at the beach but never get to meet. Guys you never get a chance to know. Once I'd gotten to know the guy behind the cute face, I'd realized Adam wasn't what I wanted. But Sam; Sam was another story. I knew what Sam was really like, and he was great. The problem was that Les thought so, too. It was beginning to sound like a soap opera.

Sadly, I got to my feet. If Sam had good sense—and of course, he did—he'd see what a sweet and loyal girl Les was, and how lucky he was that she liked him. They would make a neat couple, and everybody who knew them would agree that they belonged together. I sighed. I'd promised Sam I would return his stuff right away, but Les was there and I didn't want to butt in on their private conversation. That wouldn't be fair. I'd had my chance with Sam and I'd blown it. Now it was Les's turn and I wouldn't get in the way. But that didn't mean it didn't hurt. I blinked the tears away. It hurt like crazy.

Sunday was a pretty awful day. I mostly stayed in bed or hung around the house, telling my family that I hurt all over from fighting my way through the jungle on Saturday, which was partly true, anyway. I hurt all over, although I suspected that it was more because I couldn't get Sam out of my mind. Les called early in the morning, but Mom told her I was exhausted and she must have bought my excuse, because she didn't call back. Sam didn't call, of course. I didn't expect him to. I wouldn't have known what to say to him if he had called, anyway.

I figured that Monday was going to be pretty awful—and I was right. The first problem was that Les and I always walked to school together, and I didn't think I could stand hearing her go on and on about how she and Sam had finally gotten together on Saturday night and worked everything out between them. Or, if they hadn't really gotten together yet but were just planning to, she'd want to tell me all about that, too, and I'd have to say how glad I was that things were going to work out. I might be up to listening, but I definitely wasn't up to telling Les that I was glad she and Sam had something going. Especially if he'd kissed her. She'd want to tell me all about that, I knew. And I didn't think I could stand to hear it.

Lucky for me, Ellyn had gotten the car because she had to drive somewhere in the afternoon. So she helped me avoid Les by giving me a ride to school. And we were late, because Ellyn had spent an extra fifteen minutes in the bathroom putting on her eye makeup, so I avoided the second problem, which was that my locker was right next to Les's locker. I didn't end up arriving at school until homeroom period was almost over.

But still, being late was a problem all by itself. I had to stop by the office and get a tardy slip from Mrs. Pinkerton. Then on my way to homeroom, who should I see coming down the hall toward the computer room but Adam! He was whistling a happy tune, and he smiled when he saw me.

"Oh, hi, Maggie," he said. "Hey, I just wanted to tell you what a great partner you were on Saturday! Maybe we didn't exactly burn up the trail, but I got a real kick out of watching you handle all those crises. I never knew that girls could be so resourceful."

I stood there clutching my tardy slip, staring at him. Adam DeLong was telling me how much fun it had been to watch me handle crises? Was this guy for real? Maybe this was his way of apologizing for being such a jerk, but it wasn't exactly working.

"Yeah," he went on cheerily. "In fact, Jennifer and I were thinking that maybe the club could start actually recruiting girls. You know, make up a bunch of big posters about how much fun kids can have out in the wilderness." He winked at me suggestively. "It can be fun, you know, when you've got the right team together."

"Uh, thanks, Adam," I said hurriedly. I wasn't in the mood to even try to imagine what his idea of the "right team" might be. "I think I've had enough of the wilderness. If it's all the same to you, I'll get my fun somewhere else for a while." I turned on my heel and left Adam standing in the middle of the hallway.

I kept myself pretty busy for the rest of the morning, dodging Les and avoiding the places where I thought I might see Sam. But finally it was time for math class, and I couldn't put off the evil moment any longer. I pasted a phony smile on my face, squared my shoulders, and marched into Mrs. Mitchell's classroom, prepared to be cheerful and brave. I'd seen a show on TV a few months before where a woman who was dying of some dread disease had given up the man she loved to her best friend, and I'd cried all the way through the last half hour. It was a role I figured I could play.

But Sam wasn't there.

I looked around, feeling both relieved and let down. At first I thought that maybe he was just late, that he'd be sliding into his seat any minute. But he still wasn't there by the time Mrs. Mitchell took attendance, so I guessed he was absent. And then an awful thought occurred to me. I hadn't seen Les all morning, either. Sure, I'd been trying to avoid her, but it's kind of hard to avoid somebody who has a locker next to yours, isn't it? That is, unless she was absent today, too! Maybe Les and Sam were playing hookey together. Maybe they'd gone for a long bike ride out into the country, or taken the bus into Orlando to spend the day. Sure, it wasn't the kind of thing either one of them would normally do. But then again, falling in love can make people do crazy things, right? At least, that's what happens in the movies. I was pretty sure that it could happen in real life, too.

By the time math class was over, I'd absolutely convinced myself that Les and Sam had run off together—and maybe not just for the day, either. Maybe they'd run off together permanently. In fact, I decided unhappily, I'd better start checking the mail. Chances were good that I'd be getting one of those wish-you-were-here postcards in the next few days, signed, "Love, Les and Sam."

So when I saw Les in the hall, two minutes after class, I did a double take. "I thought you were in Orlando," I said. "Or maybe Miami or Bermuda."

"Bermuda?" Les asked. She gave me an enormous smile. "Why would I want to be in Bermuda when there's so much good stuff going on right here? Today is the happiest day of my life, Maggie! All my dreams have come true!"

I sighed. It was coming. Now she was going to tell me all about her and Sam and how wonderful it was to be in love and how he had kissed her on Saturday night and—

"And there it was, right at the top of the list," she was saying dreamily. "Today, Willow Park Drama Club, tomorrow Broadway! Roses from my fans, rave reviews from the critics, my name in lights—"

"Wait a minute," I said. "Roses? Critics? Name in lights? What's all this about?"

Les raised her arm in a dramatic gesture. "It's about being a star!" she cried. "I've been chosen to play Juliet in the next Drama Club play! We're doing *Romeo and Juliet.*"

I gaped at her. "The lead?" I repeated. "You're so happy because you got a part in a play?" A little flame of hope darted up inside me. Maybe I'd overreacted about this thing between her and Sam. Maybe . . .

"Isn't it wonderful?" she bubbled. "And it's all because of Sam Tilden! You know, Maggie, he's such a terrific guy. Why, he's the one who inspired me to get the part!"

I bet, was what I was thinking, but I didn't say it. The little flame of hope inside me went out with a brief, protesting hiss. I didn't want to hear any more about how wonderful Sam was—I knew that already. That was the problem. "Yeah," I said. "He's pretty neat. So how come you didn't tell me you were trying out for the play?" I asked, trying to change the subject.

She looked down. "Because I didn't think I was going to get the part, and I didn't want you to feel sorry for me. Anyway," she added, "you had your head in the clouds over Adam. How did the meet go? Did he like your jacket? Did you show him what a terrific wilderness guide you are?"

"It was okay," I said wearily. "If you don't count the times that Adam got a thorn in his arm or fell off a log into the swamp or got lost or bashed the stuffing out of a hognose snake." The bell rang at that minute, cutting into my sentence. It was okay, though. Maybe later, I'd feel like laughing and talking to Les about my day with Adam, but not just then. She'd found Mr. Right—and I'd picked Mr. Wrong. "Listen," I said, "I've got to run to class. I'll see you later. Okay?"

Les nodded. "Well, okay," she said. "But it will have to be *later* later. I've got an important date right after school, and I don't want to be late for it. Sam's counting on me."

"Yeah," I said sadly. "Well, you and Sam have fun."

After supper that night, I gathered up Sam's compass and canteen and the other stuff I'd borrowed and put it into a big paper bag. There was no use putting off seeing him until school tomorrow. I might as well get it over with tonight. Then I could get on with the rest of my life, and get used to the idea of Les, my best friend, and Sam, the perfect guy for me, as a couple.

I was feeling more and more nervous every minute on the way over to his house, thinking maybe I shouldn't have gone at all. Maybe Les had stayed for supper and was still there. Maybe they'd be angry if I bothered them. Maybe—

Sam opened the front door after my first knock. "Maggie, hi!"

"Excuse me," I said. "I hope I'm not interrupting you or bothering you or anything." I thrust the paper bag at him. "Thanks for loaning this stuff to me."

"Oh, that's all right," he said in a muffled voice. I could hardly understand him.

Then he sneezed, twice, very hard, and almost dropped the bag.

"Excuse me," he said politely. "I have a very bad cold." He sounded awful, and now that I looked closer I could see that his nose was red and his eyes were bleary. "Don't come in," he added cautiously, holding up his hand. "I might be contagious. I wouldn't want you to catch my sore throat."

"I'm sorry about your throat," I said. "Lemon juice with honey in it is good."

Sam nodded. "I'll try it." He looked down at the bag. "I hope you had a good time on Saturday." He sneezed again. "Listen," he said, pulling a tissue out of his pocket, "would it be too much trouble if I asked you to get my homework assignments for Mitchell's class?"

"Sure," I asked. "Anything else? I could get your history assignments, too, if you want me to. I'm not in that class, but I could ask the teacher to give them to me."

"That's okay," he said. "Les is handling history for me." He began to look a little distressed. "Excuse me," he said. "I'm going to sneeze again. I don't want to leave you standing in a cloud of deadly germs." He shut the door in my face.

So that was it, I thought as I walked

home. That was the end of my grand and not-so-glorious infatuation with Adam, and my brief love affair with Sam. The trouble was, I couldn't forget about Sam as easily as I could about Adam. I mean, I could see now that Adam was a jerk, impressed with his own self-importance. But Sam was a genuinely nice guy: sweet and kind and good-looking, exactly the kind of guy you hope you'll someday fall in love with. My problem was that I'd figured all this out too late. Instead of Sam and Maggie, it was going to be Sam and Les, and I was just going to have to try to get used to it.

So I tried. I tried all week. Since Sam was still out with his cold and Les was busy practicing to be the star of the Drama Club play, at least I didn't have to be confronted with the awful sight of the two of them standing beside Les's locker or holding hands in the hall. But still, the thought of the two of them together was hard to get used to, and when I phoned Sam every night to give him his homework, I felt like crying over the telephone. I wasn't sure I could get used to it.

Chapter Fifteen

Sam finally came back to school on Friday. He didn't say anything to me after math class, because he was too busy giving all his homework to Mrs. Mitchell. But he came up behind me in the cafeteria line at lunch and handed me a tray.

"Thanks for getting my homework," he said. "Mitchell tried to find something wrong with it, but it was all there, down to the last minus sign."

"You look better. Your nose isn't red anymore," I told him. I sneaked a look at him out of the corner of my eye. He was wearing a plaid shirt and khaki slacks and he looked very cute.

"It was the honey and lemon juice that saved me," he said with a grin. He picked up a taco and began to heap it with lettuce and tomatoes. "Hey, you haven't told me about Saturday yet. How did the orienteering meet go? Did you get to use any of the stuff you borrowed?"

I reached for a bowl of cottage cheese

and added a carton of milk to my tray. "Well, it was a very enlightening day," I said. "I learned a lot. I was really glad I had your compass. It came in handy after Adam lost his compass in the swamp. Along with our map."

Sam looked at me. "I see. So you and Adam got paired up for the day, huh?" There was a strange note in his voice.

"Yeah. We were paired up, all right," I said. I got a bowl of peaches to go with my cottage cheese. "Actually, your hatchet was very helpful, too. I used it to chop a tree limb for a crutch, because Adam twisted his ankle when he fell into the swamp after he got scared by an alligator. Then he used the same crutch to beat off a hognose snake that was attacking him—after he escaped from the alligator, of course." I had to grin, remembering the way the poor, battered snake had slithered off into the palmetto, trying to get away from the crazy guy with the big stick.

Sam looked incredulous. "You mean, a *hognose* snake? Adam beat up on a harmless hognose snake?"

"And the mosquito repellant worked great, too," I went on, enjoying telling Sam the story. "In fact, I'm afraid we used it all up. Adam forgot to bring some for himself. He didn't think he'd need any—and he wore shorts, too. In fact, there were enormous swarms of mosquitoes—we even got picked to do the *Mosquito Bay* Trail, can you believe it?"

Sam finished putting cheese on his second taco. "It sounds as if you and Adam had a *great* time on your safari." He smiled. We both picked up our trays and headed for the line at the cash register. "Are you sure you don't want to keep the compass or any of the other stuff—for the next time you go orienteering, I mean?"

"Well, actually," I said, as I paid for my lunch, "I don't think I'll stick with orienteering. I'm not really crazy about swamps and mosquitoes."

Sam paid for his lunch, too, and then he looked at me. "What about Adam?" he asked quietly. "Are you still crazy about him?"

I looked at him, surprised. Why was he asking me that? Was he teasing me? But his eyes looked very serious. "Well, to tell the truth," I said thoughtfully, "I'm not really crazy about him any longer, either."

"You know something?" Sam said. "I'm glad to hear that." He nodded toward the door. "Listen, Maggie, why don't we take our trays out to the courtyard? We can sit under the tree all by ourselves and—"

I coughed. "That would be nice," I said uncomfortably. "But don't you think you ought to, well, you know, wait for Les?"

Sam looked blank. "Les? Les Langsdorf? Why should I wait for her?"

"Well, *because*," I said. "Aren't you two—?" I stopped. "I mean, haven't you been—?" I cleared my throat and blurted, "Isn't she your girlfriend?"

Sam stared at me, and then began to chuckle. "My girlfriend? Whatever gave you that idea?"

I swallowed. "Well, because she—I mean, the two of you—" I stared at him. "You mean, it isn't true?"

Sam took my arm with his free hand and steered me toward the door. "Of course it's not true," he said. "I did spend a few hours on Saturday afternoon helping her get ready for her Drama Club audition. And she brought me my history homework on Monday after school. But she's not my girlfriend, Maggie."

"Oh," I said. Suddenly everything had become crystal clear to me: Les was in love with Sam, and was trying to spend as much time as she could with him, but he wasn't in love with her. There was a big wooden bench under the oak tree in the center of the deserted courtyard, and we sat down on it. I wasn't sure what else to say.

"Well, then," Sam said, "if we've got all that straight, what would you say about going to a movie with me tonight?"

"Tonight?" I asked. I opened my carton of milk. I was so nervous that I splashed about a third of it onto my lap. How could I go to a movie with a guy that my best friend loved—even if he didn't love her back? It wasn't fair to Les, was it? I wished that I knew more of the rules of this sort of thing. I would have to read more of Ellyn's romance novels. She had to have some new ones hidden somewhere in our room.

"I'm not contagious any more, if that's what you're worried about," Sam said. He handed me a paper napkin and took a bite of his taco.

"Oh, no," I said hastily. "It's not that. It's nothing, really. I mean, I'm not worried about anything." I knew I was babbling, but I couldn't stop. "Actually, it sounds like it might be a good idea, but I have to check with somebody first."

"Oh, your mom?"

"Well, sort of," I said. "Listen, how about

if I let you know later this afternoon?" I speared half a peach, but it slipped off my fork and onto my lap. "I could call you after school." I tried to rescue the peach without Sam seeing it, but it fell from my lap onto my shoe.

"Sure," Sam said. He bent to pick up the peach on my loafer. "If you can make it, why don't we try for the early movie? Would seven be okay? We'll have to walk, because my folks won't be around to give us a ride." He looked at the peach in his hand, and then threw it into the trash can next to the bench.

"Seven would be fine," I said happily, as I handed Sam the paper napkin. Then I thought of Les, and my happiness evaporated. "Well, maybe it'll be fine," I added, in a more cautious voice. "I'll let you know."

Les was wriggling into her gym suit when I came into the locker room before phys ed. "Either I've gained another five pounds," she said disgustedly, raising her voice above the babble of girls' voices, "or my gym suit shrank a full size in the last wash."

I looked at it. "That's *my* gym suit," I said. "Don't you recognize it? It's got my initials on the collar. It must have gotten into your locker by mistake."

"Oh." Les looked relieved. "Thank heavens," she said. "I certainly don't need another five pounds, not until the play is over. You should see my costume. It makes me stick out"—she dropped her voice—"like Marlene Mackelroy." Marlene Mackelroy is this girl in school who's unbelievably developed for somebody who won't be fifteen until next semester. All the girls envy her, and all the boys stare at her—constantly.

I found a place on the crowded bench and sat down. "Listen, Les," I said. "I've got something to ask you." I began to unbutton my blouse. "Something really important."

Miss Crickenbaum came into the locker room and blew her whistle. "Everybody on the floor," she shouted. Miss Crickenbaum can give a very good imitation of a drill sergeant without even meaning to.

"What is it?" Les asked, jumping out of my gymsuit. She handed it to me. "I certainly hope you've got *my* gym suit."

I handed her my gym bag. "I guess it's in here," I said. I cleared my throat. "Uh, it's about tonight." I stopped. How was she going to feel when I told her that Sam had asked me for a date?

"Oh, here it is," Les said, pulling the rumpled suit out of the bag. "So what about tonight? I have to baby-sit the Pain. Do you want to help?"

I took a deep breath. "I can't," I said miserably. "Sam's asked me to go to a movie with him."

Les's grin nearly split her face. "Sam? Sam Tilden asked you to a movie? Hey, that's great, Maggie."

I stared at her. "You mean, you don't mind?"

"No. Why should I mind? I think you two are perfect for each other. I've been thinking that for months now. I couldn't imagine what you saw in Adam, when Sam was so cute and so nice."

"But what about you?" I asked uncertainly. "Don't you—well, didn't *you* like him?"

"Sure, I like him," Les said. She snapped up her gym suit and began to put on her tennis shoes. "But there's somebody else I like a whole lot more." She was beaming. "And I think I might have a chance with him, Maggie. He's the guy who plays Romeo in the Drama Club play. Maybe you noticed him the other night at the swim meet. Remember the guy in the blue trunks, with the dark hair and the blue eyes? His name is Peter."

I blinked. "For a best friend, Leslie Langsdorf, you've certainly been keeping a lot of secrets to yourself. Don't you think you could have told—"

Miss Crickenbaum interrupted us. "If you young ladies aren't on the floor in thirty seconds, I'm going to give you detentions." She clicked her stopwatch and began counting. "One, two, three . . ."

Sam showed up at my house at seven, wearing jeans and a striped oxford cloth shirt. On the advice of my mother, I wore my denim miniskirt, a red blouse, and my red flats. When we got ready to leave, Frog was sitting in the front-porch swing. He was wearing my father's stopwatch around his neck, timing two ants that were climbing up the porch-swing chain.

"Going on a date, huh?" he asked, with a sly grin.

I blushed. "Frog, stop asking personal questions."

"What's so personal about a date?" he demanded. "Besides, we're related." He leered at Sam. "You going to kiss her when you get home, Sam?"

Sam grinned at me. "Oh, I don't know. I might," he said. He leaned toward Frog. "Are you taking lessons in kissing? Do you want to watch? Just promise me you won't time us, though."

Frog sighed. "It'll probably be past my bedtime," he said. "But maybe I could sit at the hallway window upstairs, and—"

"No, maybe you won't," I said hastily, blushing even brighter red. "Come on, Sam."

"At least bring me a candy bar!" Frog called as we went down the sidewalk.

"Brothers," I said in disgust, after we were out of earshot. "What a pain."

Sam reached for my hand. "Oh, I don't know," he said, wrapping his fingers around mine. I felt kind of tingly inside, but in a good way—relaxed, not nervous. It felt like the most natural thing in the world to hold hands with Sam. "They're kind of nice, sometimes," Sam went on. "I wish I had one or two. Or maybe a brother and a sister. It gets sort of boring, being an only child. When you're an only child, your parents don't have anybody else to blame things on."

On the way to the movie we talked about the relative merits of relatives, about people we knew, and about school. Sam told me that I could congratulate him, because the Computer Club had elected him president that afternoon. I told him that I didn't have anything to be congratulated for, except that I'd won the volleyball game with a last-second spike and Miss Crickenbaum had told me I ought to try out for the team. He said that maybe I should do that, and then all of a sudden, there we were, at the movie theater. I stood back a little while Sam bought our tickets, thinking how special it felt to have a boy buy my ticket at the movie—and how necessary it was, too. I still didn't have enough money to buy my own.

I really don't remember much about the movie, or who was in it. We sat in the back row and ate buttered popcorn and licked our fingers and laughed until our sides hurt. The movie was a comedy. I tried very hard not to spill the large soft drink Sam bought me, and I was successful—until almost the end of the movie, that is. Sam scooted over just in time.

"That was a good movie," Sam said, as we came out of the theater. "Are you hungry? How about a pizza?"

We walked over to the pizzeria. It was crowded with kids we knew, and as Sam and I walked across the room to a table in the back corner holding hands, I could feel people looking at us. I knew that they were saying. "Hey, look—there's Sam Tilden and Maggie Mason. Are they going out together now?" It was a good feeling to know that we were being talked about. And my good feeling kept on growing, even when I looked in the other corner and saw Adam and Jennifer sitting together. I waved carelessly and smiled, and they waved and smiled, too.

Sam studied the menu. "Maybe a medium pizza, with everything?" he asked. And then he added, "How do you feel about anchovies?"

Anchovies? I couldn't remember ever eating an anchovy, whatever that was—probably a vegetable, or maybe some new kind of cheese. But I didn't want to look stupid in front of Sam, so I nodded enthusiastically. "Anchovies? I love anchovies. Could we get a double order?"

Sam looked a little dubious. "Well, if you're sure," he said. The waiter looked at us strangely when he took our order. When the pizza came, I picked up a slice and took a big bite. But it was so gritty and salty, with such a fishy taste, that I had to spit it out.

"What's the matter?" Sam asked, looking at me curiously.

I took a big gulp of my soda to wash down the horrible taste. "Fish!" I sputtered. "Somebody made a mistake and put some sort of yukky fish on our pizza!"

Sam laughed. "But you said you *loved* anchovies," he reminded me, leaning forward to wipe a string of cheese off my chin with a napkin. "Anchovies are fish."

"Oh." I looked at the pizza. "Oh," I said again, in a very small voice. "I see."

Sam kept on laughing. "Maggie Mason," he said, leaning across the table and putting his hand over mine, "has anyone ever told you just how cute you are?" Then he handed me a fork. "A little anchovy goes a long way," he said. "Why don't you scrape it off with this?"

The moon was out by the time we walked home. It cast long, dark shadows over the sidewalk and I could smell Mrs. Hutchins's honeysuckle across the street, still sweet and heavy in the autumn air. When we got to our house, Mom was making popcorn in the kitchen. She gave us a small bowl and we went back out to the front porch and sat down on the front-porch swing. We pushed the swing gently back and forth for a few minutes, nibbling at the popcorn in the bowl on my lap and not saying anything. Then Sam scooted over closer to me and put his arm on the back of the swing. Tingles of electricity ran up and down my spine and I shivered, even though it wasn't cold. I shivered even more as Sam leaned closer and put both arms around me.

"My breath probably smells like anchovies," he said.

I giggled. "Mine, too."

"You don't mind being kissed by an anchovy?" he asked.

I shook my head. "From one anchovy to another," I began, but I didn't get to finish my sentence, because Sam's lips were brushing mine. Just then the popcorn bowl happened to slide off my lap and somersault onto the floor. Sam's right foot was covered with buttered popcorn.

"Excuse me," I said breathlessly. "Let me pick that up and—"

"It's perfectly all right," Sam said. His arms tightened around me. "I don't mind a little popcorn on my shoes. We can pick it up later. That is, unless you have to be someplace else in the next few minutes."

But I couldn't think of any place I'd rather be.

Here's a sneak preview of *Love Song*, book number two in the continuing FIRST KISS series from Ivy Books:

I looked at the trimmed lawns on Sycamore Street, with the lights going on one by one. Everything was quiet at night here—no sirens, no cars, no sounds of people calling to each other. Mom and Dad said they liked the peacefulness of Scottsdale. I didn't.

My mind drifted away from homesickness and Brooklyn to Johnny Jack. I wondered what he was doing now. I tried to picture him, all alone in some fancy hotel room getting ready for his next show as the sun set outside his window. Maybe he was feeling lonely as he picked at the strings of his guitar, working out the melody for some sad, soulful song.

That brought me into another of my favorite Johnny Jack daydreams. In it, I am walking down the street in Manhattan. Johnny Jack looks out of his hotel window and sees me. He's instantly smitten with my beauty and runs down to the street. Because he wants me to like him for himself and not his fame, he pretends he's from another country and asks me for directions.

I don't recognize him (in this fantasy I'm not a Johnny Jack fan—yet), but there's something I like about him. I offer to show him where the Metropolitan Museum is. We spend a wonderful day together, with me thinking all the time that his name is Jacques.

Jacques comes to see me every day. We go on picnics, to the movies, on long walks in the rain. We fall madly and hopelessly in love. But suddenly Jacques disappears mysteriously, and my heart is broken.

Then one day a Johnny Jack album comes in the mail. The title of it is *For Kelly*. I'm shocked to see that there is a picture of me on the front cover. I don't know what to think. The last song on the album is circled. The title of it is "A Love By Another Name."

The song is all about a girl who falls in love with someone she thinks is a poor Frenchman, only to find that he's a rich, famous rock star. As I listen, I understand. Suddenly I feel a presence behind me. I turn around and there stands Johnny Jack wearing a sad but serious expression.

"Can you ever find it in your heart to forgive me for deceiving you, my love?" he asks.

"Oh, yes!" I cry, flying into his arms, kissing his face wildly. "Of course I—"

"Look out!" a voice cried, interrupting my fantasy. "Look out!"

It was too late. I'd been so caught up in my Johnny Jack daydream that I hadn't noticed a boy on a skateboard who was heading straight for me. It was Tommy McKeever. He crashed into me and we both fell down.

"I'm sorry," I said, getting up off the lawn. "You must think I'm a total menace."

Tommy had fallen to the other side of the sidewalk. He lost the angry look on his face once he saw it was me. "What were you thinking about?" he asked as he rubbed his wrist. "You looked like you were in another world."

"I was thinking about the Johnny Jack Bellows concert next month," I answered. It was almost the truth. I was glad it was dark out because I could feel myself blushing. How could I convince Tommy that I wasn't always this klutzy? He didn't seem to mind, though.

We stood on the corner and talked for half an hour. It turned out that Tommy lived right around the corner from me. "I've never seen you walking to school," I said.

"I go early for football practice," he explained. "We have our first game next week. Are you going?"

"I don't know much about football," I admitted.

"That's okay," he said. "I'll tell you about football if you tell me about Brooklyn."

"Sounds good," I laughed, "But it will have to wait until tomorrow. I have a ton of homework."

"Okay, see you tomorrow!" he called, pushing off skillfully on his skateboard.

"Bye." I still had the letter for Kim in my hand. I put it in the mailbox and turned back toward my house. This time as I walked I wasn't thinking about Johnny Jack. I was thinking about Tommy.

Who'd have believed that a boy from Scottsdale who played football and didn't like Johnny Jack could be so nice? He was, though. He made me feel as if I'd known him for a long time, like he were old friends—and yet I felt nervous and thrilled to be near him. It was a strange feeling, but I liked it.